LAKE SUPERIOR TALES

STORIES OF HUMOR AND
ADVENTURE IN MICHIGAN'S
UPPER PENINSULA

SECOND EDITION

MIKEL B. CLASSEN

Modern History Press
Ann Arbor, MI

Library of Congress Cataloging-in-Publication Data

Names: Classen, Mikel B., author.
Title: Lake Superior tales : stories of humor and adventure in Michigan's Upper Peninsula / by Mikel B. Classen.
Description: 2nd edition. | Ann Arbor, MI : Modern History Press, [2018].
Identifiers: LCCN 2018035325 (print) | LCCN 2018056499 (ebook) | ISBN 9781615994090 (Kindle, ePub, pdf) | ISBN 9781615994083 (hardcover : alk.
    paper) | ISBN 9781615994045 (pbk. : alk. paper) | ISBN 9781615994090 (ebook)
Subjects: LCSH: Upper Peninsula (Mich.)--Fiction.
Classification: LCC PS3603.L3843 (ebook) | LCC PS3603.L3843 A6 2018 (print) |
    DDC 813/.6--dc23
LC record available at https://lccn.loc.gov/2018035325

Published by
Modern History Press   www.ModernHistoryPress.com
5145 Pontiac Trail   info@ModernHistoryPress.com
Ann Arbor, MI 41805

Tollfree: 888-761-6268 (USA/CAN/PR)   Fax: 734-663-6861

Distributed by Ingram Book Group (USA/CAN/AU), Bertram's Books (UK/EU)

Contents

Also by Mikel B. Classen

Non-fiction
   Au Sable Point Lighthouse, A Beacon on Lake Superior's Shipwreck
      Coast
   Teddy Roosevelt and the Marquette Libel Trial

Fiction
   Journeys into the Macabre

Anthology (as Editor)
   U.P. Reader (issues #1 – 3)

The Bigg Man

It was good to be on dry land. The voyage north had been ugly. He stepped off the ship onto the dock, grateful that the trip was over. Other passengers moved past, all seeming to want to hurry away from the schooner that had taken such a battering. He looked around, taking in the new surroundings.

Dock workers were moving to begin unloading the cargo from the schooner, and he walked toward the young, remote town. The town had been a spot on the map for many years but only recently had it begun to grow quickly. Sault Sainte Marie was the gateway to Lake Superior. Minerals had been found along Superior and the only way to get them out was through Sault Sainte Marie. Literally. The river that connected Lake Huron and Lake Superior had large rapids and falls, so no ships could pass without either being completely taken out of the water or their cargo transported from one ship on Superior and then to another below the falls southbound to Lake Huron. Nothing passed by here without going through the town itself.

He thought about all of this as he headed for town. There certainly would be opportunities here. He smiled to himself. McKnight's docks. He would have to remember that, after he rested up.

Ahead of him, he could see the fort, Fort Brady. The town was centered on the other side. He never did like the military. Better to depend on yourself.

He followed the dirt road around the fort and he could see the plank buildings lining the road that made up the main part of town. A saloon was what he needed. He walked past the fur company warehouse and heard the familiar noise on his left.

The sign said "Small's Saloon." It would do. He took a last look down the street at the people moving about doing those things that they thought were important at the moment. He was pleased that it wasn't him. He went through the double glass doors and walked straight to the bar. The man behind the bar walked right up. "Hello, I haven't seen you here before."

"Nope, you haven't."

"My name's Jake, Jake Smalls. What's yours?"

He ignored the question "I've had a long trip and I just want some whiskey and a few peaceful moments where the floor isn't constantly shifting. Give me a bottle."

"We don't have bottles. It's all in casks. It's easier to ship that way."

"I don't think I can drink quite that much."

"Glass or a mug?"

"Mug."

Jake went over to one of the three casks he had mounted on the bar and poured out a mug. He handed it to the stranger who took it and went to a corner table and sat where he could look out the window.

First impression was that it was a quiet place, though he had heard that it could be dangerous too. He'd done his research before he came. Sault Sainte Marie was a small town in a strategic location on the verge of a boom. There were rumors of gold, silver and copper to the west and all of it would have to come through here. If trouble wasn't here already, it soon would be. It hadn't officially become a town yet so there were no rules. The only legal control was from the soldiers at the fort, so it was wide open country with little chance of repercussions. A man could accomplish much here, legal or illegal. The Canadian border ran right down the middle of that river out there, so this could be a smuggler's paradise.

His thoughts were broken by some loud shouting and the entrance of three soldiers from the fort, this obviously not being their first saloon stop. "Smalls! Whiskey! Now!" one of the soldiers shouted at Jake. The stripes on his uniform pegged him as a Corporal. He noticed that Jake was a little on edge with this bunch. One of the soldiers seemed to notice him and nudged the Corporal.

"What do we have here? A newcomer. I think we should get acquainted, let's go over and have our drinks and introduce ourselves to the stranger here."

The stranger just looked at him and then quietly said, "I prefer to drink alone."

"You don't want to have a drink with us? Here we are trying to welcome you and you won't have a drink with us?" The corporal and his two friends moved over to his table and stood over him.

The room had gotten very quiet. The card game that had been going on in the corner had stopped. This wasn't how he had pictured his day going.

The Corporal spoke again. "My name is Corporal Ferguson. This here is McCann and James. Now, you want to be our friend, because if you're not our friend, things can be difficult around here. Now what's your name?"

"That's none of your concern."

The corporal leaned over the table, close enough that his breath was polluting the immediate air. "You don't get it. We're the law around here. We can lock you away and throw away the key and nobody is going to ask any questions. Hell, we can dump your body in that river out there and nobody's going to ask us about it." The two companions were smiling and laughing. This wasn't the first time they'd put someone through this.

The stranger leaned back slightly and said quietly, "Really?"

"Really." The Corporal sneered and looked hard at the stranger. That was when the stranger's hand went out and the Corporal's head impacted with the table top. He bounced up and flew backward, sitting on the floor. There was blood where his nose was, now flattened out and more was running out his mouth.

The two companions began to move forward toward the stranger, but he jumped up and said, "Please do. Now that your Corporal has got me started it'd be a shame to have to stop at just one."

The two looked at each other, weighing their chances while the Corporal was spitting out blood and trying to catch his breath with a smashed nose.

"Come on if you're gonna. You already interrupted my drinking. If you do it again I might get angry and I'd hate to inconvenience the fort doctor like that."

The two men, still standing, backed up, looking at the Corporal. They were obviously not used to thinking for themselves and were looking to him for some direction. "Get me up," he finally managed to blurt out. The two companions picked him up and steadied him between them. 'You haven't seen the last of me," he hissed. The blow to the head had caused some balance problems.

The stranger said, "I suggest you get him back to the fort while you still can." Someone had given them a direction. Now they knew what to do. They ushered the wobbling Corporal Ferguson out of the saloon and up the street.

The stranger finished the whiskey in his mug and brought it up to an amazed Jake Smalls. "I've never seen the Corporal handled like that. He's not going to let that go, you know."

The stranger smiled at Jake. "I'm counting on it. By the way, know of any good boarding houses? I need a good night's sleep."

"Sure. The Hopkins House. You can get coffee and breakfast there in the morning, too."

"Great," he said as he headed toward the back door.

Suddenly, Jake spoke up. "Don't go out that way." The stranger turned, slight puzzlement on his face. "I have a pet out back. He helps keep the customers honest. No sneaking out the back way without paying." He leaned over the bar and whispered to the man.

The stranger smiled, then hesitated, thought for a moment and decided he might as well get it over with. Everyone was going to find out sooner or later anyway. "By the way, the name's Biggs, Gabriel Biggs." He didn't wait for the reaction and headed out the front door and onto the street.

He went to the boarding house Jake had suggested. He had been right: clean, nice and inexpensive. His room had a view of the river, he could see the water rushing mad, crazy over the rapids. He could hear the noise of it coming through the walls. It would be good to sleep in a real bed again. He'd had enough of accommodations aboard ship on the journey.

Gabriel sat on the bed and pulled off his boots. He'd been wearing them so long it was like they'd become a part of his feet. Finally they came off. He lay back on the bed. Memories of his past came to him briefly, especially those of his old friend Andy Jackson.

* * *

He woke up with a start. There were six men in his room. There were six rifles pointed at him. His eyes adjusted, seeing the uniforms and a soldier spoke, "Sir, you are under arrest. You are to come with us to the stockade."

Gabriel sat up slowly and said, "I'd prefer to be taken to your Captain."

The soldier shook his head and replied, "Our orders are to take you to the stockade, sir."

Very slowly Gabriel reached over to the nightstand and picked up a piece of paper, "Soldier, please read this," and handed it to the Private. The Private read for a moment and then looked up. "Yes, sir, I'll take you to the Captain."

Biggs pulled on his boots and then commented, "I suppose no one brought coffee."

"No, sir," the Private answered.

"Damned uncivilized, waking a man without coffee," he muttered.

* * *

Corporal Ferguson came out of the fort's doctor's office. The doctor had given him something called laudanum. He said he'd feel better in no time. Both of his eyes had taken on a purple-black hue and his face was swollen in response to his smashed nose. He felt with his tongue — two of his front teeth were loose also. He cursed under his breath. He'd get even with that son of a...

His thought was interrupted by a soldier running toward him.

The soldier stopped and then said, "Corporal Ferguson, the Captain wants to see you in his office." If it wouldn't have hurt so much, the Corporal would have smiled. 'Now we'd see.' Ferguson was certain the Captain wanted to know what kind of charges to press.

He walked across the compound directly to Captain Tremain's office. Knocked, heard "Enter," opened the door and came into the office. He stood at attention and saluted.

That was when he noticed the man sitting in a corner, sipping fresh, hot coffee. His feet were propped up and he appeared quite relaxed.

"Corporal, you don't look so good," Tremain commented on Ferguson's face.

"Captain, I ordered this man arrested and I want to press charges for assault."

"So I've been told," replied the Captain. "I've also been told that you provoked the assault and that you're lucky the damage wasn't worse."

Biggs spoke up, "Excellent coffee, Captain."

"Thank you. Feel free to get some more if you'd like."

Biggs stood up and walked over to the pot that was sitting on the wood stove and poured out a little more while the Captain continued with Ferguson.

"Mr. Biggs here has decided not to press charges and bears no grudge." Ferguson stood, looking straight forward. This was not how he'd expected his morning would turn out. "If I hear of you ever bothering Mr. Biggs again, it'll be you in the stockade waiting for a court martial, am I clear?"

"Yes, sir."

"Also, if you ever order a civilian's arrest behind my back again, I'll have you shot. Now get out of here before I change my mind."

Ferguson turned and went out the door. He was seething with anger. Biggs, Biggs, where had he heard that name? No matter, he'd get even. He had his ways. He'd get even with the Captain too, but he already knew how he was going to do that. He'd had a plan for a while and it wouldn't be long now, the Captain would be powerless and he, Ferguson, would be in charge, rank or no rank.

Biggs left Captain Tremain's office, satisfied. The Captain had done everything Biggs had asked. But then why wouldn't he? It was all to the Captain's advantage. Biggs could do things that Tremain couldn't. Biggs wasn't hindered by nasty little things like "chain of command" and "orders." He needed a drink and some information. He went back to Jake Small's Saloon.

Jake smiled as Gabriel came through the door. "I heard you were arrested."

"It was a misunderstanding. It's been cleared up."

"Yea, I thought maybe it might be. Mug?"

"Yeah. I need to know something. Where would you hire someone of exceptionally questionable character?"

"You mean murderers, thieves, cutthroats and that sort?"

"That's the idea."

"For being here so short of a time, what makes you think we have those types?"

"The short time I spent in here." He grinned at Jake.

"Point taken," replied Jake. "There's a place. It's a saloon on the other side of the fort, past McKnight's docks up in the woods. It's a nasty place. A man gets killed in there and they just dump him in the river, no questions asked. It gets washed downstream and they never find a body. It's like they left town. Listen, Biggs, take my advice, you go in there, being a stranger, in five minutes you'll be carried out feet first and tossed in the drink."

"I've been in some pretty tight spots in my day, but thanks for the advice. I'll be careful."

"Gabriel, they don't call it the Blood and Guts for nothing."

Biggs finished his mug and went back to his room at the boarding house. He opened his luggage trunk and took out a wooden case. It was rectangular and about six inches thick. On the top was a brass plate that had an inscription etched into it: TO THE MEANEST MAN I EVER KNEW, ANDREW JACKSON. Gabriel smiled to himself as he read it.

* * *

It had happened more than ten years ago. A group of men had been walking with the President, Andrew Jackson. Biggs was one of them. Though the street was lit, there was a deep darkness that hung in the shadows. Out of one of the shadows and behind the men came a man. Even in the dim light the steel from the gun muzzles flashed, leaving no doubt to their presence. Two men looked back at the President and saw the man approaching behind him. Biggs and the other man, Senator Crockett from Tennessee, grabbed the President's shoulders and pitched him behind them while the man pulled the triggers. Nothing happened! The guns had misfired! Both men broke for the assailant, Biggs reaching him with a right cross a hair's breadth ahead of Crockett. Biggs pummeled the man senseless and bloody, but he made sure he was alive enough to stand trial. From that moment on, he had been by "Old Hickory's" side as unofficial bodyguard.

* * *

Almost reverently, he opened the case. Inside, laid in blue velvet, were what looked like two pistols, but they were very different from the usual. There was no flint, no rod attached to the barrel. Instead there was a round cylinder that revolved behind the barrel and the hammer of the pistol struck what was in the cylinder. It was a new kind of gun, one invented by Samuel Colt. It was called a "revolver" and it fired six shots without reloading. Jackson had seen this new marvel and had commissioned Colt to make 200 of them for Jackson's friends and military comrades. The shot and powder was held in a brass casing called a cap so the powder never got wet, and reloading was as simple as sliding another load into the cylinder slot. The gun was pure genius and very rare. And Biggs had two. An ample reward for having saved his friend and President's life.

But that had been a long time ago, and he had been young then. Now he was older, wiser and meaner. He reached back into the trunk and pulled out a dark brown coat. It was heavy and leather. He put it on and picked up the colts. There were special pockets on the inside that the guns fit into. Biggs shrugged his shoulder so that the coat lay on his shoulders comfortably. It hung to the back of his knees.

The last thing he pulled from the trunk was a large knife. The sheath buckled onto the outside of his coat where it was easy to snatch. He knew what he was about to do was dangerous but it wasn't the first time and it certainly wouldn't be the last. He was prepared. It was why he had been sent here.

He left the boarding house quietly through a side door, went to a line of trees and blended into the shadows of the woods. Darkness was falling and he would be able to move unseen, unheard. Like a phantom he moved past the fort and skirted the Blood and Guts Saloon. The boisterous noise drifting through the trees made it hard to miss. Biggs approached it from behind and then circled around the side, always careful to stay concealed within the trees and underbrush. Gabriel had no desire to end up trout food in the river.

It wasn't long and he sighted Corporal Ferguson along with his two companions, McCann and James. They had two others with them that Biggs hadn't seen before. He guessed they were regulars at the saloon. Ferguson was talking to them, the alcohol making them loud enough that Biggs had no trouble hearing them.

"There will be five of us," Ferguson was saying. "What I want you two to do is act like you're robbing us. We then shoot the other two soldiers and you take the payroll. We meet up later and we split it."

"What makes you think that we wouldn't just keep it all?" one of the men asked.

"Then there wouldn't be any more jobs and the three of us would suddenly get very good at describing the thieves. If we pull this off, there will be other payrolls we can snatch as well."

The two men nodded and grinned in the dim light. "We'll do it."

Ferguson continued, "We have another job for you, too. There is a new man in town. He seems to spend time at Small's place. His name is Biggs. He's the only one that can get between us and that payroll when it comes tomorrow. The three of us can't touch him but you two can use him for whitefish bait. We need him gone, I don't care how you do it."

One looked at the other. "Wanna go fishin'?"

"Let's go get some bait." They turned and quickly strode down the path into town.

Ferguson spoke to his comrades. "With the payroll gone, those men that were going to reenlist, won't. The payroll theft will cause a scandal and Captain Tremaine will be gone. This town will be ours. By the time they send another commander, it will be too late. A second payroll theft and most of the men will desert. Of course, we'll stay. Hell, it might even get us a promotion and maybe even a medal or two." He laughed at the thought of it. The laudanum he was taking for his battered face made him more conversational than usual.

A noise behind Biggs made him turn, a hand on the hilt of his knife. A very large man stood there. "Who're you and what you doin' here, hidin'?"

Biggs could hear Ferguson telling his men to be quiet, having heard the giant. The giant didn't wait for an answer and lunged at Biggs. Years of instinct, developed by moments like these, took over. He shifted left and the blade of his knife flashed in the saloon light. The giant missed and never got up. He only lay there, making gurgling sounds. Gabriel Biggs slipped into the woods.

Ferguson found the expiring body of the giant. He thought of Biggs. Then he smiled. Biggs wouldn't live out the night. Those two knew how to kill. It's what they did best. They'd bleed him for awhile, taking their time. Prolonging it. Then they'd start taking pieces. It would be a fitting end for the one that had embarrassed him so. Biggs would not be a problem.

Gabriel made his way back to Small's Saloon. He entered and Jake handed him his usual mug. Biggs took a long pull and set the whiskey down. He seemed about to say something when two men came in.

They were the ones Ferguson had hired. Biggs let out a long sigh and thought, 'Well, this is convenient.' As he turned from the bar he felt two muzzles protruding into his side and back.

Jake caught a glimpse of what was going on but made no comment.

"Out back," one of them mumbled. Biggs turned. Jake said nothing.

Biggs felt himself prodded through the door and stepped out behind the building. The three moved to a cleared area. The ground was worn and little vegetation grew. The two men circled Biggs, getting ready to shoot him. One of them gloated, "He ain't such big stuff. This was easy."

Biggs saw the shadow moving behind them and heard the low growl. The two men turned, taking their eyes off Biggs for a moment. The Black Bear stood on its back legs. It was all he needed as Biggs pulled both his guns. They fired as one. The two men dropped instantly, their heads leaking blood. Biggs looked up and saw Jake standing in the door. He'd witnessed everything. Biggs came up and spoke to him quietly, then Jake turned and went inside. The other patrons looked at him quizzically, having heard the shot. He turned to one of the younger men and said with urgency. "Run to the Fort and get Captain Tremaine. Biggs has been shot! I think he's dead."

Jake kept everyone away from the back door until a few minutes later when Tremaine arrived, followed by a couple of soldiers. One of them was McCann.

"Where is he?" Tremaine spat out breathlessly.

"Out back," replied Smalls.

"Keep everyone in here." Tremaine snapped. "McCann, Johnson, guard this door. No one comes out here."

Tremaine went out and inspected the body. Jake held his customers inside, but a couple could see the body on the ground past Smalls. The guards had an excellent view. Tremaine bent down to listen for a heartbeat. Then he looked up. "He's dead," he announced. "I don't want anyone out here. Lock that door, Smalls. I need to be able to figure out who did this."

McCann smiled to himself.

* * *

The next day, Tremaine paced in his office, then there was a knock. "Enter," he shouted and Ferguson came in. "I want you to put together a detail. The payroll comes in tonight on the schooner *Invincible*. I want you and four other men to escort it back to the fort from the dock."

"Yes, sir," replied Ferguson, "I'll take McCann, James, Johnson and LaLonde."

"Fine," said Tremaine. "You're dismissed."

Ferguson saluted, turned and left Tremaine's office. "I really dislike that man," Tremaine muttered under his breath after the door had slammed. After the payroll detail left the fort, so did Tremaine.

* * *

It was evening before the *Invincible* tied up at the dock. It had a particularly hard time against the River Saint Mary's current. Ferguson and his detail of men had waited at the dock for two hours. They were getting restless when the ship was sighted on the river. The soldiers stood, and watched the schooner tie up. The Captain stood on the side of the ship, watching everything from the rail. The sailors threw out a gangplank to the dock. He then ordered a chest brought up from the hold.

Ferguson smiled at the sight of it. His plan was working perfectly. Now that Biggs was out of the way, he had nothing to worry about. Ferguson looked at the sky. It was getting dark and it would be a dark walk back. He wondered where their new partners would actually stage the holdup.

The Captain had two of his men carry down the small chest between them. They set it down in front of Ferguson.

"Thanks, Captain, and the men at the fort thank you." Ferguson saluted the schooner captain.

"My pleasure," replied the Captain. "I like to do what I can to keep you boys in business."

Ferguson smiled and ordered his detail to head back to the fort.

They proceeded from the dock, uphill back toward the fort. LaLonde and Johnson were watching intently for trouble. Ferguson, McCann and James were waiting for their confederates to put in an appearance. As they approached a cluster of pines, two men stepped out. It was dark and their faces couldn't be made out, but there was no mistaking the gun barrels.

Ferguson said, a little indignantly, "It's about time you two got here."

He then turned to LaLonde and Johnson. "Kill these two here and then make it look like we put up a struggle." The look on Johnson and LaLonde's faces went from surprise to bewilderment. It took a few moments for it all to sink in.

Ferguson looked at the two and commanded. "Kill them. They can't be found with military shot in them." Johnson and LaLonde looked at each other, hoping the other would have an idea on how to get out of this. Both realized the other was at a loss.

"Damn it. Hurry up," yelled Ferguson, anger now starting to well up. The two hirelings stepped closer and into the light.

It was Gabriel Biggs and Captain Tremaine. Their eyes were hard when they looked at the traitors, thieves of the lowest kind. Biggs held his two colts and Captain Tremaine had another Colt revolver in his hand.

"Where's, where's..." Ferguson stammered.

"I suppose the word bear-bait doesn't really answer your question does it?" Biggs said with a smile.

Ferguson looked at McCann and James. "If we rush them, they only have three shots and they might get one of us, but not all."

"Actually," Biggs commented, quite at ease, "I believe we have 18 shots. Isn't that correct, Captain?"

"Yes, I do believe that is the number," he replied back. McCann and James looked at each other and then Ferguson.

LaLonde and Johnson were waiting for an opening. They were heartened to see their captain.

The three thieves moved together with their guns raised. They died in that moment together. LaLonde and Johnson never had time to move. It was over in a second.

Gabriel looked at Tremaine, "No Court Martial?"

"Found guilty," Tremaine grunted. He bent down and confirmed they were dead. He looked back up. "Besides, they weren't going to let us take them in. They knew there could be only one outcome, hanging or a firing squad."

Tremaine motioned to LaLonde and Johnson. "Let's finish delivering this pay." The men nodded and Biggs went with them. Tremaine would send back a detail to pick up the bodies. The payroll had priority.

After they arrived at the fort, the Captain thanked Biggs. "I appreciate all your help clearing this up."

Biggs smiled "Anything for an old friend. When you wrote me and said you needed some help, this country isn't big enough to keep me away. Besides, I was tired of the quiet life. I needed something to get the old blood moving again."

"I have to admit," said the Captain, "I had quite a start when I saw you lying there, supposedly dead. When you whispered 'pronounce me dead' while I listened for your heart, I knew you had a plan."

With the pay safely locked in the Captain's safe, Biggs decided to head back to Jake's saloon. The Captain waited for the bodies to be brought in. He smiled and remembered the days Biggs and he were working for Jackson.

He was broken from his reverie by a knock. In came the soldier in charge of the body detail. "We brought in McCann and James, Sir."

He saluted. "What about Ferguson? There were three bodies."

"No, sir," answered the soldier. "Just two."

Tremaine was startled. *Where did the body go?* he thought. They'd checked. All three were dead. Maybe some animal like a bear or a wolf had come in and dragged it off. He turned to the soldier. "Bury the two and go back and double check for Ferguson's body. Don't bury these men with the other soldiers," he ordered. "They were traitors and don't deserve to lie next to real soldiers. Take them into the woods somewhere. Leave the graves unmarked."

Biggs got his usual mug of whiskey from Jake. It was all over. The job was done. He went over to his table and relaxed. He put his feet up on an adjacent chair. "Finally I can have a drink in peace." He let out a long sigh and settled back.

The doors to the saloon burst open and a haggard and worse for wear man stumbled in. He looked furtively around the saloon until his eyes fell on Biggs. "Damn," Biggs muttered.

The man came over. "Are you Gabriel Biggs?" he asked. Biggs just looked at the man. "I need your help."

Author's Notes – The Bigg Man

I have tried to make the portrayal of the town (at the time) Sault Sainte Marie and Fort Brady accurately. Those early days of the Sault were rough and lawless. The settlers who came in those early days were both violent and deadly. They were not men to be crossed or trifled with. Saloons were plentiful and so were houses of ill repute. The streets were muddy and the buildings fresh sawn wood. In the midst of it all stood Fort Brady.

The fort was originally constructed in 1822 to deter British incursions across the St. Mary's River after the war of 1812. It was named after Col. Hugh Brady, who'd gone there to establish the fort under the orders of Michigan territorial governor, Lewis Cass. The fort was established near the shoreline of the river and was the only form of law in the region. It concerned itself mostly with military matters and mixed in domestic matters only when it affected the fort or its personnel. This left the surrounding community open to some rough and brutal individuals. The Sault was as dangerous as any western frontier town. For a time, Fort Brady housed the only school in the region and it cost to go to school. In 1893, the fort was relocated to what is now the Lake Superior State University campus. It was in operation until 1944.

Moby Pike

Call me Ishlamaki. I hired on to crew the big fishing trip. We all knew that it could be dangerous, but it was in our blood, we were fishermen. Our captain, Captain Aho, was a brooding, one-armed man. He never smiled and when he spoke, it was with snap and authority.

The name of the ship was the Peepott and she sailed out of Marquette onto the big lake, Superior. Where we were bound, I was unsure. All I knew was that we were looking for a big catch, one that those who had crewed with Aho before only whispered about. It was rumored that we searched for one particular fish. Beyond that, I knew not.

The big fishing cruiser rolled gently with the waves, but on the horizon I could see dark clouds, I hoped they weren't a foreshadowing of things to come.

A Native American named Wequik was sitting on a large Coleman Cooler, whittling on a stick. He looked up at me and shook his head. He could tell that this was my first time out. His hard eyes softened slightly as he spoke to me. "You picked a bad voyage to be starting out on."

"I've never had a chance to go out on the big lake fishing and I didn't want to turn an opportunity down," I said. I was anxious. This was my chance and I wanted to catch fish. I've gotten some big ones inland and have even had the occasional Negaunee Sleighride. That's where you get a fish so big that instead of reeling it in, you let it pull the boat around the lake until it tires enough to be brought in.

"Well, maybe this is one you should've turned down. You see, we're on an unusual trip. We're looking for one single fish. It's a monster. It has torn downriggers from their moorings and sunk bassboats that have had the misfortune to stray into his path." Wequik's deeply lined face etched a seriousness that gave me a chill. I knew that he wanted me to believe his every word.

"Captain Aho" he continued, "is the only man to have seen this fish close up and lived to tell about it. Now he sails only to catch the great white fish he calls 'Moby Pike.' Legend has it, at least, it's what the DNR says anyway, that this pike has been around for a long time. It was a native fish that lived under the ore dock by the hot ponds. As years went by and it fed off the plentiful minnow supply, it grew to huge proportions. Eventually it migrated out into Superior and it has lain off Stannard rock in an underwater cavern 350 feet down. So deep that light hasn't been able to reach it and it has grown white.

"That's what happened to his arm. He was rinsing out a beer can over the side of the boat when the great white pike came out of the water and took off the captain's arm, pulling him into the churning lake. Until the arm was severed, he was pulled deeper and deeper. He swam to the surface frantically, one arm and a stump. Aho broke the surface, gagging and choking. His boat was still floating nearby. He barely was able to pull himself back on board. From that day on he has sworn his vengeance on Moby Pike."

I was amazed and stunned at the story. I looked over at Aho and saw the prosthetic hand, which could no longer reel in a line or ever again clutch a beer. A small piece of understanding came to me.

I decided I would stick it out, and sat next to Wequik as we left the harbor. We rounded the breakwall and headed out into the open lake. Aho's eyes never left the fish finder's screen. His one arm instinctively steered the cruiser toward the Stannard Rock area. The Captain stood stock still, hardly breathing, never speaking, his obsession taking over.

It wasn't long and we could see the light tower on Stannard Rock. Aho spoke finally, and it was a tone that made us jump. "Set the Downriggers."

We all got to work, lowering the steel lines to 300 feet. "We're at 300 hundred feet, Captain," the mate shouted. The captain nodded and continued to study the fish finder.

After several passes, something hit. The downriggers released and the reel began to sing. Aho's expression never changed. He knew it was a Lake Trout, a big one, but not the great white pike.

The 35 pound fish was reeled in and released. Nothing was gained from the three-hour fight it took to get it. Personally, I was thrilled, but the experience had to be done as quickly as possible because the captain wanted to be on his way. Everything but the great white pike was a waste of time to him. The line was reset and we were again churning the water, resuming our search.

The giant rock of Stannard was our companion as we circled and circled, waiting for the massive shape to move from the bottom. The day wore on, with us throwing back trout after trout. There were even a couple of Cohos in there, as well. Again, nothing but the pike would do for Aho.

Suddenly, the boat tilted. Aho jumped from behind the wheel. The fish finder alarm went off and a huge shape could be seen rising from the bottom on the viewscreen. Moby Pike had taken the bait!

Fear came over me before I knew it. It was obvious we'd hooked something big. Very big! The downriggers bent and the back of the boat threatened to dip below the surface. The motor let out a squeal as it was pulled in against the direction it was running. "Sum Bitch," yelled Aho. "We've hooked him and this time we're gonna get 'im."

I could see the life spring into Aho. My native friend looked at me and shook his head. "This is gonna be the end of us. He'll shipwreck us to get this pike." I knew the truth of it as he said it. Aho's obsession wasn't going to let him give up until he got Moby or Moby got him.

Aho cut the engines and the boat was jerked backward. We clutched onto anything solid for a grip. The cables stretched, plowing the stern through the waves, and then suddenly they went slack.

The boat sat rolling on the gently rising water. The wrenching on the boat had put the fish finder on the blink so we were blind to what was going on below us.

Everything was quiet and still. Too quiet. We all stood waiting, watching. Had he snapped the line and gone off, or was he waiting, resting up for the big flurry? We didn't know. The reels had locked up from the force of the Pike, making them useless. We simply stood, looking back and forth at each other.

Off the bow there came a disturbance on the surface. Something that wasn't there before, something unnatural. I shouted, "Captain! Off the bow, something moves."

"It's Him! He rises!" shouted Aho. I felt myself starting to tremble. Somehow, I knew this would be it.

We could see the disturbance getting closer and closer. I could make out the dorsal and tail fins cutting the surface, shark-like. It kept coming closer and closer. Aho shook with excitement as his quarry was once again in sight.

The giant Pike came at the boat, his snout and side colliding with it. He rolled, tossing the boat to one side. The gunwale dipped, taking water. I dove towards the high side, instinctively trying to counter the upset balance. I looked over the side and I saw the huge red eye of Moby Pike staring at me as he rolled. The white scales glistened in the clear water. I knew terror.

I looked around at the rest of the crew. They had the look of doomed men. They knew that the boat wouldn't be able to take much more. Aho grabbed a fish gaff with his good hand and ran toward the downriggers.

Moby had once again disappeared below the surface. The downriggers began to twist and jerk. Cracks appeared in the hull below. "He's tangled in the lines," shouted Aho.

Wequik ran for the wire cutters to snip the cable, but Aho stopped him. "Belay that. I'll not give up so easily. I've got him and I'm gonna get him."

The back of the boat shook violently and we knew that the captain was mad. Once more Moby rose to the surface and slammed hard into the back of the boat. As Moby broke the water, jaws open, teeth gleaming, Aho slammed the fish gaff into the pike hard, hooking Moby securely. The momentum of the fish knocked the captain off balance. He fell into the water between the downriggers.

The prosthetic arm hooked one of the cables that was twisted around the body of the pike, and then became hopelessly entangled. The crew scrambled to try and grab their captain, but it was of no use.

We all saw him in the clear water as he disappeared below. The crew stood back, realizing that Moby was heading for the bottom.

"We have to cut the downriggers loose," yelled the mate. The command was too late. As I dove for the snips, there was a loud bang and then a sickening crunching and tearing. It was the end.

The back of the cruiser tore out and the Lake Superior water poured in fast. There was nothing left to do but jump overboard. We all grabbed life jackets and jumped.

I swam away from the boat as quickly as I could, not wanting to get caught in the undertow of the sinking wreck. Once more I saw that telltale disturbance at the surface as Moby again came back to finish his destruction.

As he surfaced, I saw something attached to the upper dorsal fin. It wasn't long before I could make out Aho, tangled in the downrigger cables, destined to be forever pursuing the object of his obsession. Moby swam, circling the cruiser. I could see Aho's good arm flapping as the fish swam, sort of a mock wave, maybe beckoning other daring fishermen to finish the job that he'd started, to follow him in pursuit of the Great White Pike.

Moby swam, creating a vortex in the water that pulled the ill-fated boat to the depths below. That was the last that I saw of the rest of the crew, I know not their fate. I floated for awhile and then I was able to grab onto something that was floating. It was that cooler where I had first met Wequik, my Indian friend, the one who had tried to warn me. I hoped that he was alright.

I hear tales once in awhile, when the other fishermen come in. Some claim to have seen it. Some even say that the figure of Aho clings to it still. As for me, I've never again ventured out into the lake. I don't think I ever will.

Bullets Shine Silver in the Moonlight

I knew she was trouble when she came through the door. It was obvious that she wasn't from around here. I stood behind the counter and watched her walk toward me. Hips with a drumbeat, that's what she was. Black dress slit up the side, black hat and spiked shoes, perfect blonde hair cascading down her slender shoulders, everything about her spoke city. She wasn't the kind of thing you saw very often up north.

She slid up to the counter and onto a stool. She sat so that I could get a good view of leg from the slit in her dress. Yes, this one was quite a dame. She leaned over the counter onto her elbow, offering me other vistas to view with her magnificently low cut dress. "I need your help. There's a terrible man following me and I think he wants to kill me." her rough voice showed a tone of desperation.

"Please hide me. He's not far behind." She gave me the wide-eyed help-me look and I was hooked like a brook trout on Hemingway's line. Besides, she had aroused my curiosity. This was Grand Marais, Michigan. These kinds of things don't happen every day.

"In the back," I said, and showed her into my little windowless office. She'd be safe here. No sooner than I had gotten back to my counter that a mid-sized man, obviously from the city, walked in. He sported a nice suit, hard-bottomed shoes and a felt hat. He was definitely from down south.

He strode up to the counter. There were thin scars across both cheeks. "I want the broad that just came in here."

"No women in here." I smiled back at him.

He leaned menacingly over the counter. "I know she's here. I watched her come in." He spat a little as he spoke.

I leaned toward him. "I told you, she isn't here." His scars started twitching in frustration. I had him where I wanted him and I knew it.

"Give me the woman or this could turn into a very bad day for you."

I stared back into his yellowed, bloodshot brown eyes. "Look out that window...across the street. See that bartender over there. That's Charlie. He watches over here and if there's any trouble, that bar will empty out and come right in here and take care of your overdressed ass." I waved. Charlie waved back. "Also, I should probably let you know that there's a .38 under this counter that is currently pointed at your expanding waistline. Now, you can leave or we can settle this in any way you choose. Personally, I don't want to have to clean up the mess. But, if you insist, you won't be the one on the happy end."

His scars were really twitching now. He wanted to try something with me so bad he could barely control it. It was obvious that old Scarface was used to getting his way. He was used to pushing people around and now someone was pushing back.

Finally, he backed away. "Mister, you just bought yourself a whole lot of trouble. I hope she's worth it." He turned and went out the door.

I hoped she was worth it, too. There was something going on here. This was a lot deeper than it looked. I went into the back to find out what the dame's story was. She sat there, and her eyes had adopted the frightened mouse look. "Is he gone?"

"For now, but I expect not for long."

"What am I going to do?" Her lips pinched, her eyes worried, but all the time she made sure I had an adequate view of her assets.

I knew she was trying to drag me into this. Actually, it was too late. She had already dragged me into it. Where I was concerned things were getting pretty deep already. There was a lot more behind this and I was determined to find out what it was.

"First thing you're going to do is tell me what this is all about. And who the hell are you anyway?"

"I'm Rayna Daye." She began to wring her hands as her story tumbled out. "It's my husband."

"What, Scarface is your husband?"

"No, Scarface just works for him. My husband is a rich man."

Not much of a revelation there.

She continued. "He used to own one of the biggest breweries in Milwaukee. A few years ago, it was bought out by Miller. It was a good and sizable payoff, but, apparently, it wasn't good enough. The money has begun to run out. Now he's discovered a new scheme. He's buying Sable Lake."

"That's impossible!" I said. "It's owned by the Feds. It's a National Park. He can't buy it."

"That's where you're wrong. My husband is well connected. He knows which hands to shake and whose pockets to fill. He's finally bribed and blackmailed the right people to where the sale is nearly final."

"So what does that have to do with you? Why's he trying to kill you?"

"I have the evidence. The payoffs, names, dates, numbers. I have it all."

I digested what she'd said. It was like a two-day-old pasty from St Ignace. It wasn't sitting too well. I simply couldn't believe that someone who looked like her was here for some idealistic intent on saving the neighborhood. There had to be something more in it for her. It was still too sketchy.

"How does your husband expect to make a bundle off Sable Lake? It's a nice place, but hardly a goldmine."

"Think of it. Property values in Grand Marais are shooting up by leaps and bounds. With the size of Sable Lake, turn it into lots and there's millions to be made."

"Why come here? Why not the authorities? Any agency that can do anything is back down south. Take it to Washington, not Grand Marais."

"You don't understand. Too many are in his pocket. I don't know who to trust. I thought if I came here, to Grand Marais, the town itself could help stop this."

This still wasn't sitting right. It didn't make sense. It was too defeatist. Why would a woman want to upset her husband's plans when she herself stood to profit quite well in the deal? No, something stunk here, but my instincts were telling me that I needed to get her out of here. Scarface was lurking somewhere and I didn't want to get caught when I wasn't ready.

I went back out front to the counter. Through the front window the full moon was coming up across the bay. I could see the silhouette of a man in front of it. Scarface was waiting. He was watching the place looking for a glimpse of Rayna. I took my .38 out from under the counter. This could get nasty.

Back in the office, I motioned to Rayna. She stood up, still impeccable. "We're going out the back. I saw old Scarface out the front and I'm hoping he's working alone."

"He probably figured I wouldn't be this much trouble and I wouldn't find anyone to help me."

"Apparently brains aren't a requirement for working for your husband."

I slowly opened the back door. I had the .38 ready just in case. "Listen, Toots, we're going to have to make a break for my truck."

Her face fell. She looked horrified. "TRUCK!"

"You're up north baby, 4-wheel drive."

"At least you've got a gun."

"It's the U.P. *Everybody* has a gun."

We went out the door and flattened ourselves against the wall of the building, sidestepping toward the truck. "When you get in I want you to get down. When I start this up. I expect Scarface is coming after us. Hopefully, he wasn't smart enough to leave his car close. Let's go!"

If we could get out of there, I knew where I could take her that she'd be safe, at least for awhile until I could make some plans and get closer to the bottom of this. Her story reeked like road kill on a hot day.

Her heels clacked as she scurried down the sidewalk and tried to get into the truck. We didn't have time for this. I flew into the driver's seat and reached out. She grabbed my hands and I yanked her in. There was no time for delicacy, bullets could be flying at any moment.

The second the truck started I threw it in gear.

I was right, Scarface came running around the corner of the building. I could see him reaching inside his coat to pull out his iron.

I had the truck squealing as I pulled a u-turn in the street between my store and the saloon. I let off a couple of rounds from my .38, more to attract attention than to hit our pursuer. Sure enough, in my rear view mirror, I could see the bar emptying out and Scarface putting his gun back in his coat.

The last time I did anything like this was back in '89. The DNR was chasing me. Those were the days.

Rayna had adjusted to the truck as best she could. I saw her reach inside her bodice and pull something shiny out. It was a flask. "Want a tug?" she asked.

I took it, feeling the warmth in the metal. I smiled to myself and swallowed some of the bourbon. It gave a whole new meaning to keeping it close to the chest.

Down two backroads and an alternate way to the backside of town and we were there. The old Boarding House. Rayna would be safe here. The old woman that ran the place, Tess, wouldn't let anything happen to her. Nobody would look for a high-class dame like this in an old boarding house. This would buy me some time to set some things up.

We entered through the back where there was no light. Tess met us coming through the door, a shotgun pointed at my chest. "Well, there's trouble if I ever seen it." She lowered the gun. "Can't be too careful with all of the commotion going on."

Tess was about 5 foot 3 and all white. White hair, white slippers and white robe, all except for the gun, which stood out well against the white. She was also tough as nails. I could count on her to not let anybody get past her. Rayna would be safe until I could figure out what her game really was. Every instinct in my gut was telling me she was either lying or keeping something from me. Her story just didn't add up.

First I had to take care of some business. I had to make plans, had to set some wheels in motion. I had to return to the saloon. Before I got back into my truck, I decided to reload the .38. I didn't want to be caught short if I ran into Scarface. Interesting, as I took out the shells, even in their brass casings, bullets shine silver in the moonlight.

* * *

I went in through the back door of the saloon, then quietly slid into a corner, so that I could look over the joint. Scarface was at the far end of the bar. There were too many people for him to try anything. I knew most of them, he was a stranger and with those city duds, I knew he wasn't going to get any help. If he had a teaspoonful of sense, he'd stay put, but he really hadn't been too smart so far.

"Charlie," I shouted. Scarface immediately looked up and spotted me. Charlie came down to me and smiled. "What was going on out there?"

"See that guy at the end of the bar? City Boy?"

"Yea, you want I should throw him out of here?"

"No, I want you to keep him here. As long as you can. And by all means don't let him use the phone."

"Too late, he already made a call, just a bit ago." Too late. I looked at the clock. I figured I had eight to twelve hours. It was enough time, but I'd have to get things rolling now.

"Charlie, first I need a shot and a beer."

Charlie was the best bartender I knew. It wasn't that he could fix a drink like no one else, but it was because Charlie was a full service bartender. Charlie had connections. Anything that needed to be done, Charlie was your man.

I downed the shot in a swallow and chased it with the beer. "Charlie, I need you to locate the Indian for me, fast."

"He was in here earlier, but it's been a few hours now."

"I need him." Charlie could see I was serious.

"I'll send someone to shake him loose." Charlie went down to one of the younger patrons and said something to him. He ran out the door.

"And, Charlie, I need you to call the Finn. Tell him there's trouble in the Marais. Tell him, tell him Luigi's coming. He'll understand."

Charlie nodded. "You got it."

He got me another beer and a shot because he knows I never have just one. It's bad luck to let your cocktails stand alone.

"Send a drink down to City Boy at the end of the bar, will you?"

"Sure. It's funny, you know, he keeps asking about a beaver lodge at Sable Lake. I asked him, 'Which one?' I mean, you know, there's got to be 20 or 30 of them out there. I told him, I says, 'You don't want to go messing around with the beavers out there. The Feds, they don't like anyone messing around with the beavers. They fine you big, they do.'"

Charlie took a glass of wine down to Scarface telling him it was from me. He glowered at me, I could see his scars twitching. I smiled. Now that things were set in motion, it was time to go back and quiz the dame.

I decided to go out the front, better visibility. Once again, exercising his brain, he stepped out in front of me. He stared into my eyes, hard scars twitching, spitting as he spoke. "Hell's coming to your little town, Bub."

I stared back. "Hell can't survive here. It's too cold!" I pushed past him and out onto the street. I hate that. Stupid people are unpredictable. I would have to watch my back with this one.

* * *

I headed back to the boarding house to get some more information from Rayna. I walked in and Tess was sitting in her rocking chair, blanket over her legs. It was hard to tell that there was a double-barrel shotgun under there with her. "Room six," she said.

I knocked our prearranged signal and I heard her husky "Come in," from behind the door. She stood there in one of Tess's robes. It never looked better. As usual, her appearance was perfect, striking. The flask was in her hand. "Care for another tug?"

I started to feel Hemingway's trout hook again so I shook it off. I took a slug of the bourbon and got back on track. "What's the rest of your story? There has to be more to it than what you're telling me. All I see is where you stand to lose in all of this."

She looked at me with the mouse eyes. "I grew up here," she blurted out. "I hated my life here. My dad and uncle were commercial fishermen. Everything smelled like fish all the time. It got into everything, my clothes, my skin. It was terrible." Her bottom lip quivered and her eyes began to tear. "I hated it so much I ran away at 15. I went to the city. I even changed my name to Rayna Daye. I used to be Louise Lindquist. I tried to get as far away from that life as I could. To this day, I can't eat fish. I guess I'm just a red meat kind of girl."

"That still doesn't explain anything."

"Sable Lake was my refuge. It was the only place I could get away from things, the kids teasing me, my home, the smell of fish. I can't see him ruining it. Besides, my husband is an evil man. His name is Victor Carlotti and he's one of the most ambitious men there is. He does what it takes to get what he wants. He knows I have evidence that can send him up the river. He can be nasty and cruel. He controls many men in all the right places. He has to be stopped and here is as good a place as any. Back here, full circle."

"Why would Scarface be asking about beaver lodges at Sable Lake?" I asked.

"I don't know."

I looked into the imploring pools that were her eyes. The moist lips pouted, quivering slightly. Wow, this dame was good. I was feeling the trout hook again. "Where is this evidence you said you had?"

"In your office. I found a loose board at the base of the left side of your desk. There are account records and two tapes of conversations my husband made."

"I have an idea of someone I think I can trust. He can look into the Fed side of this. Maybe bring this whole thing down on your husband's head and clean up some politics while we're at it." I knew that was what she wanted to hear. She needed me to take it hook, line and sinker. There was still more here than she was dishing out.

"Well, sweetheart, I better go and get that evidence before it falls into the wrong hands."

When I reached my truck I found the Indian sitting there. He grinned. "What kind of trouble have you got us into now?"

"Big," I replied. I explained to him what I needed him to do. He nodded and got out of the truck. I drove off to retrieve Rayna's evidence.

* * *

For a G-Man, Jason Goodson is a decent guy. He was with the park service, but he had risen up through the ranks and knew which feds he could trust. "Do you think you can get this into the right hands?" I asked.

"Yea, I have some ideas."

"We're going to have to do this fast if it's going to work."

"Are you sure all of this is legit? I don't want to be making these kinds of allegations and have it come back and bite me in the butt." He rubbed his bearded chin.

"That's why I need Fed help. They can run the handwriting and voice analysis. It could very well be rigged evidence. I know this babe isn't giving me the full scoop."

"Alright, I'll look into it."

"Do it quick because I got a feeling things are going to blow up big in a few hours."

"I'll take care of it." Jason got back into his Park Service truck and took off.

I headed back to my shop, the .38 always at hand. I went inside and stood behind the counter. I could still see her coming through the door. She certainly was something. I turned around and the Indian was standing there. I about jumped out of my skin. "I wish you wouldn't do that."

"And miss the opportunity to see that. Not a chance."

I was jumpy enough as it was without the Indian playing tricks on me. Actually his name was Ed Surefeather. He was the best tracker and silence man I knew. When Ed tracked, it was a work of art. He could find a trail when there was none. He gave true meaning to silent as a ghost. The only time anyone ever knew he was around was when he wanted them to. He was one of my most trusted friends and I had entrusted him with the most important job, keeping an eye on Rayna Daye.

"She's gone!" He looked at me expressionless. "Slipped out of the boarding house."

"Gone where?" I couldn't believe it.

"Well that's the thing. You gotta come see this."

I just looked at him dumbfounded. A dame like that, she can't go anywhere unnoticed. "Where would she go? I mean she stands out, you know."

"You just really have to see this. When she came out of the boarding house, I wasn't sure it was her. She wasn't quite how you'd described."

"What do you mean?"

"Well, you just have to see for yourself. Drive out to Sable Lake."

We bounced down the back roads in my truck. The Indian stayed quiet for the ride and when I would press him for more information, he would only say, "Just wait. You've got to see this for yourself." We drove past the boat launch at Sable Lake and across Toes Creek, heading south. It was a trail I didn't often take and I soon found out why. Mud and muck were everywhere and eventually the Indian looked at me and said, "Park it here."

We hiked through the woods until we reached an obscure clearing on the south end of the lake. It looked like there had been an old hunting camp or small homestead standing there at one time. The Indian looked at me and whispered, "Quietly, slowly."

Ed moved like he was a part of his surroundings. Me, I moved like an elephant. I cracked a branch and he just glared at me. You know that look, the one that says stupid white guy.

Ahead I could see what looked like an old foundation, a sharp rise in the grass, but no building. We moved closer to it. I stopped and listened and I could hear some noise. Movement and boards cracking, and there was this metallic clinking.

I drew my .38, but the Indian saw me and waved me off. Without words I knew what he was telling me. I wouldn't be needing it.

We crept up on the foundation. There was a cellar where the building had been. Someone was down there working, bent over, lifting and piling. Sweatshirt, jeans and sneakers, but there was no mistaking those long blond tresses. Rayna, looking more like Louise than the immaculate Rayna, was working on...on gold! She was surrounded by gold! There were gold bars, ingots, everywhere, pounds of it, maybe hundreds of pounds.

I looked at the Indian. He looked back. "I told you, you had to see it."

At the sound of his voice, Rayna looked up and saw us for the first time. I looked at her. "Never trust a dame."

I always knew there was a lot more to this caper than she was letting on. It was time to find out the whole story, the real story.

"Okay, Baby, it's truth time. Give it up. Why am I about to be shot by a mob from Milwaukee, while you're sitting on a pile of gold?"

She began her tale. "You specifically? Luck of the draw. It just happened to be your joint I walked into. There was nothing more thought out than that, but it appears I made the right choice. You make the biggest Private Dick look bad."

She continued, "I told you the truth when I said I was the daughter of a commercial fisherman. What I didn't tell you was that I went to my father when he died. He was sick and in the hospital. He was lying on the bed, a terrible hack in his cough. He knew he was dying and needed to talk to me. He told me a story about him and my uncle."

"One day they were fishing off Au Sable Point. They usually avoided it because there were so many wrecks out there that they often got their nets caught. This time was different. They got their nets caught alright, caught on gold bars. They couldn't believe it when they brought up two gold bars. Suddenly fishing had finally paid off."

"They marked the spot and went to Munising to get some underwater equipment. They brought up a ton of gold bars. 2000 pounds are sitting here. It was an old civil war schooner called the Marie Jennie and it went down around 1870 and no one had a clue as to it whereabouts, especially since there were no survivors."

"My father and my uncle worked quietly and moved all of the gold here to my uncle's Sable Lake camp. My father and uncle agreed to hide it and leave it lie because they felt it would look too suspicious if they started bringing gold bars to the bank.

"Then, the Feds bought Sable Lake. Everyone had to sell. There was no choice.

"My father tried to get out there, but then he fell sick. He's been sick for years and now, on his deathbed, he told me about this secret fortune. 'The gold is at the beaver lodge at Sable Lake,' were his last words.

"The only problem was, as my father finished his story, I looked up and Viktor stood in the doorway of the hospital room. He'd heard the entire tale. He just didn't know where the beaver lodge was. Only I knew that. That's why he wanted to buy Sable Lake so badly. He could buy the property and tear the place up until he found it. Then he'd kill me to shut me up or at least follow me until I showed him where the gold was and then kill me. Either way, the key words here are kill me! He tried to get the location out of me, but I wouldn't give it up. I got away from him, so I ran here as quickly as I could."

It made sense to me. It certainly wouldn't do to have Carlotti's wife's body turn up in his own backyard. He'd be much better off to get her far away from home and then do away with her. Hell, we had swamps. They weren't going to find the body.

With a flourish of her arm, Rayna answered the last big question. "Welcome to what used to be the Beaver Lodge. My uncle's nickname was Beaver and this was his cabin. Hence, the Beaver Lodge."

"What happened to your uncle?"

"Strangely enough, he drowned off Sable Point in a storm just a couple of years after they found the gold. By right of salvage and by right of inheritance, this is my gold."

I couldn't argue with her there. It was hers by right, but if the Feds discovered it on their property, they'd claim it. Of course there was also the dilemma of the Luigis hot on our tail. They shouldn't be far from arriving.

It was a few hours later when I drove back into the saloon. Carlotti and his men should already have arrived, but everything looked quiet. I recognized most of the vehicles outside of the saloon.

Leaning against the bar was a tall, lanky man camouflaged from head to toe. I grinned to myself. I'd have to remember to tip Charlie big for this. It was the Finn. "I hear ya got trouble."

I shook his hand and ordered him a beer and a shot. "I need to set up a big surprise quick."

"Already set. Charlie gave me some of the lowdown, so I've already set up a surprise for the Luigis. Big surprise." He had that self-satisfied look with a little impish smile of mischief, or maybe that was just the shot and beer, but I had the reassuring feeling that my luck was holding out. I knew I could count on the Finn. "I want to hear the rest of the story. Obviously Charlie isn't completely in the loop."

"I'll let you in on the whole thing when it's over. Right now I'm expecting a caravan from Milwaukee all bent on killing me."

"This has got to be woman trouble."

"That's a big bingo."

"Is she worth it?"

"It appears she is."

"Well, like always, I got your back covered."

The Finn and I went way back. We'd known each other a lot of years and had pulled one another from quite a few scrapes. His real name was Clyde and he was a U.P. Finlander and proud of it. For me there wasn't a better man to have watching your back. The Finn was militia.

Out the front window of the saloon, I could see it was getting dark. There was a glow on the bay where the moon would soon be rising. On the corner I could see Scarface, smoking, pacing and waiting. It wouldn't be much longer. They were already several hours late, which meant they were rounding up a lot of heavies all because of me. I felt so flattered. There could be a small army of Luigis about to invade Grand Marais.

I pointed out Scarface to the Finn. "Watch that one. He's not too bright."

"That's what Charlie said, too. Gene pool the size of a mud puddle."

"With him, I think the puddle dried up."

Then it happened. They rolled into town, a caravan of black limos. There were ten of them and they came down the hill onto main street, filling it. I nodded to the Finn and the two of us walked out of the saloon onto the sidewalk. The Finn was looking all around, checking everything and every angle all of the time.

Limo doors opened and black suits stepped out on the street, all of them with the tell-tale weapons bulge under their arms. Scarface ran to the head car.

When he stepped out of the car, it was easy to tell who Carlotti was. Impeccable dress, groomed and manicured, but the real thing was how he carried himself: confident, authoritative, in control.

Scarface spoke to him. I couldn't make out the words, but I'm sure I was the subject of the conversation as he kept pointing at me and working himself into a fit. Carlotti listened and then turned toward me.

Carlotti moved across the street and his men moved away from the cars to converge on me and the saloon. It was just what the Finn had been waiting for. He whistled. The buildings came alive, everything moved. I knew what his surprise was.

For years there had been the rumor, but I knew that they weren't rumors, they were truth. The Finn was a commander for the F.L.A. the Finnish Liberation Army. They were everywhere, a group that stood ready for times of dire need. They were a secret of the Upper Peninsula, ready to protect their homes in case we ever have to secede from Michigan and become our own state. The F.L.A. could be anyone, anywhere, they could even be the guy that's making your next pasty.

Well, I thought, *a small army to deal with a small army*. I was confident again, Carlotti's men hadn't noticed the weapons that pointed at them from the roof of the market, the saloon, my store, from behind the buildings, and the fifteen guys that had camouflaged themselves as sand in the lot across the street.

Carlotti pointed at me. "You and I have business. You've been interfering with mine and I need to make corrections."

"No, I don't think so. Your business kind of landed in my lap, so I'm cleaning it up."

"You can go outta here in peace or in pieces," the Finn shouted with a grin. "Personally I prefer the pieces. It's been a slow week for me."

"What, now I gotta put up with another one sticking his nose where it doesn't belong?" Carlotti responded.

Scarface leaned over to his boss, "See what I mean, boss? No respect. Let's just shoot 'em."

"Oh, please try." The Finn grinned. He was getting excited. His men could get some practice out of this yet. All it was going to take was one person to make a move and Grand Marais would be a war zone.

That's when I heard the siren and saw the flashing blue and red lights on top of the green and white truck. My last trump card had arrived. It squealed to a halt and Jason jumped out, gun drawn, but shielding himself behind his door. "Viktor Carlotti, I'm Federal Officer Goodson, and I've got a warrant for your arrest."

It appeared Rayna's evidence had been authentic. Carlotti whirled and stared at Jason.

The Finn looked at me and grinned. "Your idea?"

"What do you think?"

"Not bad."

That's when it happened. Scarface yelled, "They ain't taking you, Boss, and they ain't taking me." He reached inside of his coat for his gun. The gun barely cleared the holster. At least thirty bullets hit Scarface at the same time, evenly grouped, in the chest.

"Nice shooting." I said.

The Finn nodded, "We've been working on that."

"Told you he wasn't too bright."

"You were right."

"Hope he didn't reproduce."

The rest of Carlotti's men stood frozen, dazed at the swiftness of Scarface's demise. I looked at the riddled body. Interesting, blood shines black in the moonlight.

Jason came up and put the cuffs on Carlotti. He smiled at me. "I think I'm going to get a promotion out of this." I could hear sirens in the distance where Jason had backup on the way.

I looked at the Finn. "Cocktails?"

"It would seem to be in order," he replied.

I put my arm around his shoulder and we headed for the bar. "I suppose it's time I told you what this is all about."

"It all started out when this blonde walked through my door," I began.

"Doesn't it always."

"No, sometimes it's a redhead or a brunette. Anyway..."

* * *

Carlotti ended up doing time in a federal pen along with several of the politicians he'd purchased. Rayna Daye, who has now changed her name back to Louise, is somewhere out on the west coast, Beverly Hills, I'm told. There's a rumor going around town that Charlie received a really large tip, one he isn't claiming, but rumors in small towns, you never know what to believe. The Indian just purchased a huge tract of hunting land. The last time I saw the Finn, he had brand new camo clothes. He says they are readier than ever for secession. Me? I'm still working in my store, but I have a really large yellow retirement plan working for me. Dames, ya gotta love 'em!

The Encounter

Looking up at the night sky, he sees the multi-colored lights streaking across the Aurora Borealis, enhancing and blending with it, yet making itself plainly independent from the exhibition of nature. A tree- and ground-shaking boom accompanies the streak. This is the fourth U.F.O. Karl has seen in his life. "Maybe it's something from K.I. Sawyer Air Force Base," he mutters under his breath. "Sawyer's always putting strange looking, noisy things into the air."

His feet become tangled in a gnarled pine root, causing him to fall onto his hands and knees, he's watching the sky so intently. Now undergrowth and the leafy ground is all he sees. A large fern gently slaps him in the face. He glances back up in time to see the thing in the sky disappear behind the tree line, but misses its direction of travel.

Karl mulls what he's seen over in his mind. It couldn't have been a meteor because he made out separate distinct different colors. The configuration hadn't looked familiar. After seeing so many of the base jets, they are an easily recognizable sight. Traveling to the air shows had been an annual affair for him and his family for years so he was acquainted with some of the experimental aircraft displays. This still baffles anything he can recall. It just doesn't fit.

Starting faintly so that Karl barely notices it as he stands back up, a glowing light grows on the skyline, gradually becoming a brilliant orange. It startles him as he brushes off leaves and pine needles from his slightly throbbing knees. One of his driving forces is his intense curiosity, as it is with most people. The glow looks reasonably close, so Karl, without any hesitation at all, decides to investigate. Besides, one of those hotshot flyboys could be in serious trouble, or possibly it's a fire starting. The materialization of this thought causes him to half-jog through the dark woods.

Less than an hour later, Karl is staring at the weirdest object he's ever seen. It is nothing like the experimental aircraft he'd watched at Sawyer. Nor is it like a flying cigar or disc-shape, like most U.F.O. witnesses describe seeing. It doesn't look like any of the U.F.O.'s he'd seen either.

Thinking about it, Karl assures himself that whatever it is that he's looking at, it could never possibly fly. It doesn't fit the laws of flight as he knows them. But then, he's no expert either, just an unemployed iron miner from South Republic, Michigan. The object in front of him is smoking and steaming from extreme heat. "Surprised the woods isn't on fire," Karl mutters to himself. "Thank God for all the rain."

The object is about seventeen feet in all directions. It isn't round and it isn't square. It appears to have been put together by randomly assembling various scraps of metal without using an obvious pattern of any kind. It baffles Karl completely as to what it is, what it does and even why it is. Long metal tentacle-like objects protrude out in eleven directions that Karl can count. He isn't sure, but there can be more on the opposite side. Karl pictures it as a mechanical Gorgon.

He watches from behind a tree, deeply intent on the thing and what it might do. One thing Karl knows for sure, this isn't anything that comes from K.I. Sawyer. The possibility of danger to his life surprisingly never crosses his mind. Fascination seems to block all else out. His curiosity is in complete and blinding control.

Suddenly, his inquisitiveness gets a boost. Sounds begin to emanate from the metal monstrosity. There is a sucking like that of a high powered vacuum cleaner, which is followed by some clicking that makes Karl think of relays switching. Slowly the appendages move and stretch. One on the left dips until it contacts with the ground, and slides along, leaving an oval rut behind it. Karl shifts himself for a better viewing advantage. The metal arm then lifts and returns to its original position. Another, on the right this time, moves and locates a tree. Karl hears what he thinks might be the sound of some type of drill. His suspicions are confirmed when the tentacle withdraws and a small wet hole is left as a scar. One arm on the top clips some leaves and draws them within.

More relays click. A stone is crushed by another arm and the shards are taken in. Karl's eyes widen at this. Appendages shift, taking and picking all that is within reach of the amazingly mobile tentacles. Mosses, dead leaves, ferns, nothing within its reach is left untouched.

Without realizing it, Karl is now standing in full view, no longer hidden by the tree that he had curiously crouched behind. The nagging and sometimes controlling curiosity got the best of him. Caution and care are gone. Fear and dread of the unknown is gone. He simply watches the thing in front of him, fascinated. It's a mistake, one he will remember.

Karl is bathed in an intense red light before he can react. Instinctively he tries to jump back into his hiding place but finds it impossible to move. His muscles refuse to obey his brain's urgent commands. He is trapped and caught. Internally he berates himself for his lax stupidity. How had he let himself get into this position?

Now the tentacles move toward him. In his mind's eye he remembers the drill into the tree, the clippings of the leaves and the crushed rock. God, what if the machine tries to give him the same treatment? Desperately he pleads with his muscles to cooperate. He is no longer curious, just frightened witless. The mechanical arms slowly surround his body. Terror wells up inside as contact seems only a second or two away; involuntary muscles still function as they should. Karl feels his body becoming coated in cold sweat. Mentally he recites the Lord's Prayer. His mouth refuses to respond for a vocal version. Just the sound of his own voice would be of some comfort to him. Somebody else's would even be better. *I couldn't have been the only one to see this contraption come down,* he thinks to himself at the same time knowing full well that this is one of the sparsest populated sections of the entire Upper Peninsula. He probably is the only one to see the thing.

All of these thoughts go through his head in an instant. In the next instant the first metal arm touches his face. Involuntarily his head jerks as he experiences a small dizzy spell. A coldness, followed by a numbing, flows into his face. A brief prick is the only thing he feels. More cold and numbing. Gently he is pierced in each location. The arms, legs, midriff, all receive the touch. Karl is unsure whether he is being hurt or not. A small bead of blood gathers on his face where the arm withdraws. Each one withdraws likewise, immediately after the procedure finishes. When all have broken contact with Karl's body, the light switches off.

Feeling almost immediately returns to his body. A grateful to be alive but at the same time extremely terrified Karl leaps behind the tree that was his previous shield. Lying there in the musty smelling leaves, he checks himself to see what damage the machine caused. There is none that he can see, other than the minuscule droplets of blood. He feels no pain whatsoever and the slight dizziness in his head is probably his own doing. The only pain he can locate is from when his earlier fall. Turning, he looks at the strange device once more, but is excessively careful not to expose himself again. He had gotten away lucky, he is certain, and he has no intention of pushing his luck.

He is just in time to see the metal tentacles retract and disappear inside the main body. Once more the thing seems lifeless, inert, silent. Nothing happens for a couple of minutes, then the bottom begins to glow green and gradually changes to orange. Behind the tree, a wave of heat washes over Karl that forces him to his feet. He runs to avoid becoming cooked. He turns as soon as the heat is no longer pursuing him, and sees a bright streak of light shoot from the woods into the sky, leaving behind smoldering, but not burning, vegetation where it had been.

Breathing hard, Karl plants himself on a mossy log to collect his thoughts and make some sense out of the chaos racing through his mind. What happened? What was it? Could he ever tell anyone?

He tries to regulate his breathing to calm down. Slowly the pictures come to him. He remembers the National Geographic magazine articles along with P.B.S. television specials and it all fits into the proper perspective. He had been too curious and frightened before to put it all together. The memories of the Viking Lander on Mars sampling, tasting and photographing the planet, the exquisite beauty of Voyager passing Saturn and Jupiter while it learned, recorded and transmitted. Earth's wondrous interplanetary probes. Everything is very clear to him now. What he witnessed was like Viking and Voyager, a probe, a sample taker that collects information about other worlds sent by some other form of life. What kind of life, he can only imagine, but some intelligent race obviously.

Karl looks at the sky with all of its flashing and glittering stars, each with their own possibility of life. He smiles. Now he truly knows without any doubt that the human race isn't alone and at the same time he knows that they have something in common, something shared: curiosity, the drive to investigate. Karl walks home, feeling very good about life.

The Wreck of the Marie Jenny

I was sitting in Shutey's Bar in Calumet, Michigan when this old man came up and started talking to me. He said his name was Captain Jack Talbot and he had a story to tell. "I've never told anyone this, but I have to get it off my chest before I die. I'd be obliged if you'd let me bend an ear so that I might rest easier in my grave. It'll be a restless slumber as it is."

I told him, "Alright," and ordered another brew since I could tell that the tale might be long. There was also a sense of urgency in the old Captain's voice that told me that this was of grave importance to him.

Captain Jack's Tale:

It was 1871. I captained a schooner named the *Marie Jenny*. We sailed out of the Keweenaw Peninsula hauling copper ore to Sault Sainte Marie. We had a reputation for being fast and efficient and I knew the Lake better'n anyone. We'd just arrived back in port for another load. I went to the shipping office to get the particulars on our next shipment where I was informed there'd be none this time around. I was to ship out immediately for Iron Bay with my holds empty. There I was to meet privately with a Mr. Peter White, a local speculator who apparently had interest in virtually everything in the area. I was to dock at Marquette where he would enlighten me as to the nature of our cargo and its destination. I was also informed that I was to tell no one of our destination and we should depart in the middle of the night.

Of course this struck me as odd, but orders are orders and they are always for a reason. I rounded up my crew to get them back to the *Marie Jenny* before dusk, which was no easy task. They had, of course, scattered among the saloons as soon as we had docked. Most grumbled, disappointed, but they all returned, being a crew of unwavering loyalty and depth of character.

We set sail well after midnight as it tends not to get dark until late during the fair months. By morning we had rounded the Keweenaw and were well on our way to the Huron Mountains. By the light of the next morning, we navigated our way through the treacherous rock outcrops of Iron Bay into the docks of Marquette. Then it was a small town but growing quickly due to the discovery of iron to the west.

No sooner had we tied up at the dock when a messenger came telling me that Mr. White wanted to see me at his private residence. His home sat perched on a ridge overlooking Marquette harbor. The building itself was impressive, made out of large sandstone blocks, trimmed in wood from the area. Its size was overwhelming, but then I was used to a schooner cabin as a home.

The messenger led me into the varnished and polished house and guided me to Mr. White's study, where the man himself waited impatiently. As I walked in, he seemed to have been pacing. The messenger announced me and immediately retreated, closing the doors to the study. Mr. White invited me to take a seat and he wasted no time getting to matters at hand. He had a reputation as a no nonsense businessman.

"Captain Talbot," He began, "I'm told you're a man of integrity and unimpeachable character. A man that can be trusted to do a job and keep it to himself. I'm also told that you have one of the fastest and finest ships on Superior, is that correct?"

"Yes, sir, it is," I answered, wondering where all of this was going.

"What I'm about to tell you can never leave this room, is that agreeable?"

I nodded.

He reached into his waistcoat pocket and rolled some stones out onto the top of his desk. They flashed in the light and I knew immediately what they were. Gold nuggets!

"I'm currently president of the bank here and one of the companies that we finance has, shall we say, come into a discovery. So far we've managed to keep it a secret, but I don't know how long that will be possible. I want you and your ship to carry a shipment of this to the Soo. So far we've managed to secretly smelt around 2000 pounds. If you agree to this, it'll be loaded up in crates marked iron.

I've several dock hands hired and waiting. They've been informed that it is pig iron bars so they won't look too closely. If word of this got out, I suspect your voyage might be short-lived."

"I'm certain that you're right. A fortune like this might inspire some serious cut-throating. Mr. White, I have a fine crew, one that I stake my life on every time I sail, but this puts them in a danger that the copper never did. A cargo like this could easily inspire piracy."

"Captain, all I can say is that I've made every possible precaution. The rest is up to you. I can assure you that when you complete this voyage, you'll never have to make another. You and your crew will be paid handsomely for your risks."

I leaned back in the chair and thought about it for a minute. White's reputation was impeccable and I believed him when he said that everything possible had been done to maintain the secrecy of the voyage. "Alright, I'll take your cargo. Send word to get it aboard. I'd like to sail as quickly as possible."

He smiled through his thick beard. "I was hoping you'd say that." He leaned over the desk and stretched out his hand. I took it with pleasure and felt the iron grip. It was then I truly knew him to be a man of his word and honest. A lot can be told from the grip of a handshake.

I rose to head back to the *Marie Jennie*. I was nervous about this and I wasn't afraid to admit it. The only problem was who could I admit it to? I was sworn to secrecy.

I arrived back at the dock and boarded my ship. I went straight to my first mate, Angus Stewart, a Scot of unfailing nerve. I'd seen him singing into the teeth of the worst gales Lake Superior could muster. He smiled through his red beard. "Cap'n, what're yer orders?"

"We load shortly and we set sail as soon as we're stowed and secure. I want no time wasted, but make sure everything's shipshape and tight."

"Aye, Cap'n." Angus set to supervising the loading. It wasn't long and the wagons arrived with crates marked "Iron." Angus shouted to his men and the ropes began squeaking and squealing as the crates were raised off the carts and then lowered into the holds. The crew knew their positions and their duties and the loading went quickly.

Then I saw it. I cursed under my breath. I hoped none of the dock-hands saw it too.

A board on the side of one of the crates had broken and was hanging loose. I knew if I shouted, it would only draw attention to it and, to my horror, I could see the edges of the ingots, their color clearly visible. Then too, Angus saw. He looked up at me and quickly replaced the board. He made sure that was the next crate loaded. Again he looked back at me. Though he didn't speak, I knew he understood everything.

I studied the dock, but I couldn't be sure if anyone had seen or not, but then, how long that board had been loose was a mystery. Angus came up. "They're stowed, Cap'n."

"Angus, double the watch and make sure the men are close to their guns. We may need them."

He nodded. "Aye, Cap'n, we'll keep a sharp eye."

"Cast off, set sails, the sooner we're under way, the sooner we're done with this."

It was dusk when we cast off. The gold was secured in the hold and I had every member of the crew with eyes to the water in all directions. We weren't going to be taken by surprise just in case someone had gotten wind of our secret.

The Lake Superior breeze filled our sails and I felt the familiar roll of the deck as the *Marie Jenny* went full speed to the east, leaving the Iron Bay behind. She was a fast ship and could make good time to the Soo, but looking aft, behind me, I could see trouble brewing.

Not of the kind I had been expecting, but the kind that spelled the demise of so many of my fellow sailors. The western sky was black and rolling: a mean summer storm was coming. We steered due east, and all the while I called orders to the men to keep her full with the wind and maintain an eye on the horizon. The more I thought about it, the more I thought that that board on the crate of gold had been deliberately broken to see what the contents really were.

Angus came up hurriedly. "Cap'n, tha' storm is moving fast and we can't weather it out here in the open."

"I know that. If we make full wind, we should be able to hit the lee of Grand Island and ride it out in the bay there. We just need to round the north point. Keep the men on those sails, but don't let down your guard on the watch either. I've a feeling this storm ain't the only trouble brewing."

"Aye, I think yer right on that, Cap'n." I hoped I wasn't.

The *Marie Jenny* plowed ahead with the storm chasing us hard. We could hear the thunder rumbling to our aft and the waves of Superior had started to build, the prow now splashing the deck as my *Marie* broke through the waves. The men scrambled but they all knew their jobs. This wasn't our first time scrambling for shelter and it certainly wouldn't be our last. I had the best crew and the best ship on the Lake.

Ahead in the twilight, I could see it looming, the north cliffs of Grand Island. We just needed to get around the point into the bay the Indians called Trout. The bay was lined with cliffs and we would be protected from the wind and the waves. It also wasn't where another ship would expect us to go. Most Captains would sail straight for the harbor of Munising, just beyond William's Landing into the shelter there. If by chance someone was chasing us, we might lose them this way.

I shouted over the wind, "Douse all lights." I wanted us to disappear into the dark. We'd sailed this section of Superior so many times that we all knew it in our sleep.

One of the men on watch came running up. "Captain Jack, there's lights aft, I think we have a shadow." I brought up my eyeglass and watched our rear horizon. Then I saw it. It was only a flash, but it was enough. Ship's lights! We were being chased. I only hoped my ruse would work. With our lights gone, they could only guess which direction we took.

The roar of the waves crashing on the rock cliffs suddenly died as we entered Trout Bay. The storm was still there but the quiet calm of the water made it feel like we'd sailed into another world. "Angus!" I shouted. He came running up quickly. "Bring her about and drop anchor. I want us to face the mouth of the bay. If our shadow figures out where we've gone, I want us ready to sail out before they can come about. Keep all lights doused. I don't want them spotting us if they sail by the bay either. Double the watch and keep them armed. We sail as soon as this blows over."

"Aye Aye, Cap'n" Angus went off to carry out the orders. I went off to my cabin.

That night, as I lay in my bunk, the thunder rolled like I've never before heard it. It would go on and on, seemingly endless and then, when it finally would fade out, another would start and then roll and roll and roll. It echoed inside those cliffs and boomed with an intensity that could be felt. It was a thrilling storm. I got little sleep, but I didn't mind.

I must have dozed because I woke with a start. Everything was quiet. Someone was pounding at my door. I rolled out of the bunk. It was Angus. "I think it's over Cap'n. We're starting to see stars overhead."

"What's the time, Angus?"

"4:00 a.m., Cap'n."

"Get the men up and ready to sail. We might be able to get a start with what little darkness there's left." I followed Angus up on deck and could see a slight glow on the horizon even at this early hour. We'd have to move to get past the east channel before we were spotted by our shadow, which was probably anchored in Munising Bay with a clear view to the cliffs of the Pictured Rocks.

"Weigh anchor, set sail," I shouted to the crew. The light breeze caught our mainsails and the *Marie Jenny* once again began cutting through the water in the pre-dawn.

We passed the east channel in the twilight of morning and the watch never caught sight of our shadow from the night before. Maybe we had outfoxed them. I quietly smiled as we entered the dreaded shoreline of the Pictured Rocks, the Castle off to our starboard. The sun came up in the east, hot and blazing. The wind died. The sails went slack.

I cursed under my breath. We were dead in the water, though the current was still carrying us in the right direction, just not very quickly. At least if the other ship were still in pursuit, they'd have the same problems, unless... "Damn!" I swore. "Keep an eye forward." I shouted to the man on watch.

"I am, Captain Jack, but it looks like we're heading for a fog bank."

"Angus" I shouted. "Put Peterson forward with his rifle." Peterson was the best shot among us. I didn't like the way this was going and I had a bad feeling in my guts.

We entered the fog with all hands on deck, eyes straining through the mist to see anything moving that might be another ship. We were well along the cliffs nearing the Grand Portal. Once we got around it, hopefully we'd be able to pick up a shift in the breeze and get back under way.

A slight breeze moved the fog and I could see the Portal for a moment and there was…something else. I only caught a glimpse. It looked like a bow behind the Portal. I couldn't be sure, but I wasn't taking any chances. "Hard to the larboard," I told the helmsman, Dupre. He cranked the wheel. The sails rustled with the change, sending us out into Lake Superior, away from the Portal. It was slow moving with barely a wind, but we made way just the same.

"Peterson, look sharp to the starboard. Keep that rifle ready."

Past the Portal I saw movement in the mist. I had been right. Our shadow had been hiding behind Grand Portal. Somehow they'd gotten ahead of us and were waiting. Now they were going to try and wreck us on the rocks and then salvage the gold. The mist got thick again and I lost sight of her. At least now I knew for sure. They were there and they were after us. So much for White's secret shipment.

Suddenly, out of the fog to the larboard came the ship. It was on a course to ram us, sending us towards the rocky shore. Dupre cranked hard on helm, but she was slow to respond. "Peterson," I shouted. "Their helmsman."

He took the shot and pitted the cherry. Their helmsman dropped like a stone, pulling the wheel with him causing the wrecker to turn sharp. Their captain scrambled to grab the wheel, but the ships were sideways to each other. Something fell next to me.

Angus suddenly appeared on a dead run, picking up what fell. It was a stick of dynamite! He threw it overboard aft and it exploded as it hit the water. Another landed on the deck and Peterson grabbed it and threw it back. This one blew as it hit the deck of the wrecker, bringing down its mainmast. She sailed away from us, crippled and slow.

Out of nowhere, the wind picked up and suddenly our sails billowed. Dupre looked at me. "Capitaine Jacques, the wheel doesn't move. Our rudder is jammed."

The *Marie Jenny* was picking up speed and we had no steering. We were heading due east, but we needed to drop anchor and fix the rudder. That was when I heard the other crack. The one that sent shivers up my back. We were in no position for this, another storm.

Dupre and I grabbed the wheel and strained, trying to free it. It wouldn't move. When Angus had thrown the dynamite over the stern, the explosion had somehow damaged the rudder. Angus came up to lend a hand, but even with the three of us, we had no luck.

The wind was picking up fast and the deck started to heave. More cracks and thunder danced overhead, and I knew we were in for a big one. I looked forward, watching the bow rise higher and higher only to fall into the ever deepening troughs as the swells surged, tossing the *Marie Jenny* harder and harder.

Water splashed over the bow, soaking the men on the forward deck, and all the while the three of us wrestled with the wheel, first turning it one way and then the other, hoping and praying we'd free it up. I shouted to Angus and Dupre over the ever increasing cacophony of the storm to keep trying. I was going below to see if I could see what was jamming the rudder.

I went below deck. Holding on as the ship pitched and tossed. I made my way down the short stair and into my cabin. I flung open one of the windows in the stern and leaned out. The *Marie Jenny* went down into a swell and the water almost came into the window and then just as quickly it was on its way back up. My timing would have to be perfect as I climbed halfway out and hung myself out the window to the waist. As the stern peaked the swell, I could see that the explosion had forced the rudder into the hull, wedging itself into broken boards.

I pulled myself back in as the ship dropped into another swell, some water following me in this time. There would be no repairing the rudder, at least not in this storm. There was the problem of the broken hull boards as well, we certainly were taking on water in the holds. Again I cursed under my breath.

I fought my way back to the deck and then up to Dupre and Angus. "Give it up, it's not going to come free." The wind had shifted to the north and the swells were beginning to batter the ship from the side. The deck was starting to tip back and forth. "Angus, have the men rope themselves to something. If this keeps getting worse, I don't want anyone getting washed overboard."

We were sailing fast, out of control on an unchangeable course. I pulled up my eyeglass to see if I could tell our position. Everything had gotten dark, along with the tossing and the rain and spray, so I couldn't make out any details. Then, a quick flash of lightning and I caught a glimpse of shore. We were little more than a mile off and were past the cliffs. Tall trees covered the shoreline. Another flash and I saw the mouth of a river. a sick feeling filled my gut, dread overwhelming me.

The *Marie Jenny* raced ahead fighting the squall valiantly. She rose and fell, all the while tossing and pitching. Maybe, I thought, just maybe. She might be going fast enough, if she doesn't draft too deep, if we were on the top of a trough we'd ride over. I said nothing to the men, I'd have my answers soon enough.

Inside I was angry. There was a fury rising within me that only Superior's wrath was going to quell. My instincts had told me not to take this cargo and I had ignored them. Now...

The *Marie Jenny* rose up on the swell and again fell deep into the trough. I heard the sickening crunch. My world fell apart. She rose again, only to fall once more amidships, and my *Marie* broke her back. We'd hit Big Sable Point, the sandstone reef that ran six feet underwater, two miles north into Superior. The river I'd seen was the Hurricane, which told me we were heading for Big Sable. Big Sable had been the end to many that had sailed before and now it was the end of my *Marie Jenny* and possibly to all of us.

I saw Angus coming towards me, slipping on the deck as the ship rolled to its side. The look on his face told me he understood that we were done for. "Every man overboard, swim for shore. Make sure they're cut loose and swim for it. Save yourself, man."

The order was given and I saw them going over the side. Some went voluntarily some not, simply swept away by the waves pounding the stranded and quickly disintegrating ship. I could hear it snapping and cracking amid the roar of the storm. I resigned myself to the sickness and sadness of it all. Of course I would stay with my dying *Marie Jenny*. It was my duty. I felt an inner calmness as I held onto the ship's wheel while Superior battered me, trying to shake me loose. I was a rock in my position and my resolve. Captains go down with their ships, that's what we do.

I knew many of the men wouldn't make it. They would never be able to reach shore with the churning and boiling that was going on around us. Then, through the spray and the mist, I saw Angus, still aboard. He came at me across what was left of the deck. He had that look in his eye and that grin. God, he was going to do something that most men would consider not well thought out.

"Get overboard," I shouted and then he leaped, only not over the side. Instead it was towards me, catching me about the waist. The momentum took us both over the side and we plunged into Superior together.

I came up spitting, sputtering and cursing. "What the hell... Angus." I could feel him behind me trying to pull me toward the shore in that chaotic water. I yelled, "I'm supposed..." I got a mouthful of water. "...to go with the ship!" I went under for a second and came up choking. "What's the matter with you?" I screamed while hacking water out of my throat. He kept pulling and ignoring me, which was making me angrier. Between the waves and the deluge I could see the *Marie Jenny* breaking up. I should've been aboard with her. I should've gone down. I had lost everything, my ship, my cargo, and my crew. They were drowning around me. Going down with my ship was all I had left.

I struggled to get away from Angus so I could drown in peace, get it over with, but his grip was like iron. Finally I gave up and let him have his way. I didn't want him, Angus, the loyalest man I ever knew to die, too.

Through it all we reached shore, alive! I don't know how he did it, but he did. Most men couldn't have pulled themselves through a sea like that, but he had pulled two through it, successfully. We lay there on the shore for a while, catching our breaths, retching the water we'd swallowed. It was a long time before we moved, exhaustion getting the better of us.

After we'd rested and regained our breath, I looked at him, I needed my answers. "Why? Why didn't you let me go down out there?"

He spat out his answer through gritted teeth. "Men died out there. Men we've sailed with, good men, the best, and they're dead. Cap'n, there's an unbalanced account here and it's up to us to settle it."

Angus had a hard look in his eye that I'd never seen before. It gave me a chill. Angus was angry to the bone and he wanted a reckoning. I understood. I looked out into Superior where my ship had been. My ship, my crew, my reputation, all were at the bottom of Superior. Angus was right. There were accounts to be settled here. "Alright Angus, I'm with you."

First I decided to get a fire going. If one is smart, even in a storm dry wood can be found. Using the bow and stick method we got our first flames and then a decent fire to get through the night. I hoped that if there were others that had survived the storm, they'd see the flame and reunite with us. Three others joined us eventually. Sadly, the rest had perished. Dupre, Peterson, and Williams shivered around the fire, silent.

It was a long night. None of us actually slept. We were angry and sad, mourning our companions and in stark disbelief of the suddenness of our situation. The remnants of the storm swirled around us and it ended just before dawn. With the light we began moving, working the stiffness and the wet out of our bones.

We had no provisions and we were hungry, but fortunately, our situation could have been worse. About five miles away was Grand Marais harbor. We knew there was a trading post there and we'd be able to get some food and drink, then we'd try to decide on our next move. As the sun rose we began our trek along the shoreline. Above us was the Grand Sable, the giant sand cliffs that announce the entrance to the Grand Marais.

It quickly got hot, though with Superior beside us, the want of water was not an issue. The day progressed on. Our walking was slow going, the sand and piles of round rock hindering us. The fish flies covered our legs. Angus and I kept the lead. We spoke little, determined to reach the harbor, and then make plans. Toward dusk, we reached the end of the sand cliffs and, again, the woods began, which was the landmark for the west end of the harbor.

We would have to cut through the woods and then skirt around the bay to the east end where the trading post stood. In the distance we could hear the whine of a saw singing. The saw mill, the only thing that was on the west end, was working. Angus and I led the way through the woods and around the mill. As we once again reached the shore and the south side of the bay, a surprise waited for us.

I grabbed Angus and pulled him back into the shrubbery. "Stay down. I don't want them to see us." I motioned for the men behind me to get down and hidden.

"It's them, ain't it, Cap'n?" Angus whispered.

"Yeah." Floating in the center of the harbor was the wrecker, the ship that had attacked us and sent my *Marie Jenny* to the bottom. As I thought about it, their anchorage made sense. A remote harbor with a sawmill at the end. Perfect place to get a new mast cut without too many questions and too much notice. Of course the storm was convenient as an excuse for damage.

"Men, back into the woods," I ordered. We moved back into the wooded covering and formed a small circle. We'd unintentionally discovered these villains and I intended to take advantage of our luck. Since they were making repairs, they'd be staying for a couple of days.

"Listen, men, we've been pushed and we've been pushed hard. Their mistake is that we survived. I've a plan that'll even things, but it's killin' that it'll be about, are you with me, men?"

Dupre spoke up first. "Capitain Jacques, 'tis a matter of honor with me. Our comrades lost. Our ship. I do this. If I were the only one left alive, my path would be the same."

Peterson next. "Captain, I don't like this kind of business, but we've sailed together too many years not to sail with you now."

Williams. "If it's vengeance we're after, then so be it. I'm all for it, in the name of our brothers."

Angus smiled. He had been ready since he dove off the sinking ship.

Our advantage was surprise. I was certain that they figured we were dead, long drowned by the storm. My only consolation was that I knew the *Marie Jenny* went down far enough offshore they'd never be able to recover the cargo of gold.

I looked at the men. "First thing we have to do is get some food and provisions. We'll make our way to the trading post, but we stay hidden. I don't want that crew to know we're here. I have a plan. If we stick to it, we can settle some accounts." I looked right at Angus when I said it. "And in the process we might be able find out who was behind it all."

Angus spoke up." Cap'n, I know you kept this one close to the vest, but I think we deserve to know exactly what happened back in Marquette."

I related the conversation I had with Peter White and how he had assured me that his security was impeccable and right up until now I still believe that he truly thought that. Somewhere in his midst there was a rat that he was unaware of. Someone who was in cahoots with the ship and crew that was now anchored in front of us. The only way to find out who it was, was to get the name or names from someone in the crew.

We trailed through the woods until we reached the creek across from the trading post. A small boat was beached there, a shore party from the ship, no doubt, picking up some supplies to take back to the crew. I had the men stay hidden while we waited for them to leave. Our impatience was driven by gnawing hunger that had set in heavily.

Fortunately we didn't have long to wait. A group of men came out of the trading post and began loading supplies into the boat. My blood boiled at the sight of them. I wanted to cut their throats right then, but I knew that wouldn't do. We wouldn't be able to get them all.

We waited quietly while they rowed back out to the anchored ship. Angus and I decided that we would be the ones to go into the trading post to get food and the supplies we'd need for the days ahead.

We collected what little money we had in our pockets after jumping ship, hoping it would be enough to get what we needed.

We slipped through the door, hoping to create as little visibility to the harbor as possible. Angus looked at the proprietor and grinned. "Angus, you old dog."

"Angus, is that you?" the proprietor replied. He came out and the two clasped hands in a handshake that only true friends exchange.

"Angus, you old sea-rat, what have you been doing all these years?"

"Couldn't live without the deck of a ship under me. What got you way up here?"

"Remember Barbeau from Mackinaw?"

"Peter, yeah."

"He sent me over here to run this post for him. He's got himself into business, big over in the Soo. Been expanding all over Superior."

I stood and looked at the two, a bit at a loss.

"Cap'n Jack, this is an old friend of mine from Mackinaw. Angus MacDonald."

"Always happy to meet a friend of Angus," I replied and continued. "What do you know about that ship anchored in your bay?"

"Not much. This is the first time they've been here. They said that they needed to repair storm damage. I will say they're going to be going at it pretty hard tonight. They bought a lot of whiskey." I thought about this information and smiled to myself. They were going to make it easy for us. This fell into my plans better than I hoped.

"Angus," I began and got two replies.

"Cap'n?"

"Yes, sir."

Well, I wasn't used to that. "MacDonald, we need provisions for a few days, but they need to be light, packable." I laid what little money we had on the counter hoping MacDonald would accept it." We need some long-bladed knives. We'll be heading across country. Things can get thick this time of year. Angus...Stewart, Get everything together. I'm going to take some food back to the men and let them know. We'll meet you out back to pick everything up." I nodded toward the money. "That enough?"

Angus MacDonald smiled. "You're gonna owe me a favor."

MacDonald gave me some jerky, dried fruit and some fresh milk from the cow he kept behind the trading post.

I left and went back to the rest of the crew. They were waiting back in the woods, impatiently, hungry, and chewed heavily by the bugs. I passed out the food and fresh milk. It wasn't long and I could see the life come back into their faces.

As soon as we were done, we roused ourselves and met Angus with the rest of our provisions out back of the trading post. "I talked with MacDonald and he insists we were never here. Hasn't seen me in years. Figures I've drowned by now."

I looked at him and grinned. "It's good to have friends in remote places. Get this gear stowed and we'll get ready to settle some of those accounts. I don't think we'll find a better time."

Angus grinned back. "Aye, Cap'n." I could see that Scottish blood of his was hot and ready for the work ahead.

Using the woods for cover, we backtracked around the bay until we were as close to the wrecker ship as we could get from the shore and still stay under cover. We cached our provisions and packs, keeping only the long bladed knives we'd gotten from MacDonald, and settled in to wait for the darkness of night.

We could hear the laughing and shouting coming from the ship. They had obviously wasted no time in dipping into their supply of grog. I was hoping, no, counting on a hard drinking night for the crew. I had explained my plan to my men.

The mosquitoes feasted as we waited there in the darkness. In the distance the yells and occasional gunshots continued on through the night. It was only toward dawn that silence again filled the bay. Still we waited. We wanted them in a sound, drunk sleep. By the time the scum realized it, it would be too late.

Just before dawn, I roused the men. It was time. Silent and careful, we waded into the bay. The water reflected the blackness of the night.

Then we were swimming. Soon we reached the anchor-line. As we climbed aboard, the men were like silent wraiths, silent wraiths with long, gleaming knives.

Two men were loudly snoring, one on a roll of rope and the other on a pile of nets. It was good to have men on watch you could count on. Glad they hadn't tried to sign on with me. The mistake would cost them...dearly.

I motioned to Angus and Dupre to move in and silence the watchmen. They moved along the rail until they were alongside the sleeping men. They laid their knives across their throats and whispered in their ears as their eyes fluttered open from the feel of the cold steel. Angus and Dupre were quick. The words I told each of my men to say were out and the guards' throats cut before they could utter a sound. The five of us regrouped. I cut a long length of rope from the pile under the dead watchman and coiled it around my shoulder.

The men spread out and headed below deck. I went astern to the Captain's Cabin. As I suspected, the door was unlocked. Luck still being with me, the hinges squeaked, but didn't wake the soundly sleeping captain. On the floor, a large empty bottle lay on its side. I crept forward, expecting him to wake at any moment. He didn't.

I reached the hammock and uncoiled the rope. As he slept I tied him. Through some miracle, though I believe I should never have succeeded, I got him secure, wrapped up in his hammock. His eyes fluttered open as I laid the knife across his throat. The cold steel always does it.

I slapped him across the face to wake him up. Both his eyes opened this time and he growled. I pressed the blade harder, causing a thin trickle of blood. Slowly he began to realize his full plight, completely bound.

"What do you want?" he whispered. I felt his throat bounce against the blade.

"You don't recognize me, do you?"

He slowly moved his head back and forth in a "NO," afraid the motion would send my blade deeper. "I'm the Captain of the *Marie Jenny*. I didn't die with my ship, but most of my men did. I want answers. Who told you about our cargo? Who's behind you?"

"Go to Hell," he spat. I reached out and with a quick stroke of my blade I held his ear in my hand.

"Ever see one from this point of view? Funny looking things, aren't they?"

His eyes got big. And he choked, "No." I whittled on him for several minutes, digging deeper all the time. A piece here, a piece there, a close up view of a toe. Finally he talked. He told me everything. He told me the name of the traitor. Then I stuffed a cloth in his mouth.

Though I had done some horrible things to him, things that would haunt me all my days, my vengeance was not complete. I cut down his hammock and he slammed to the floor. I took a length of rope and tied it to a beam in the cabin, the other end around the wrecker captain's neck. I eased him feet first out the closest cabin window. Carefully he was eased down until the rope was taut. I made sure he didn't drop, I wanted him to strangle slowly.

I watched for a moment as he jerked and twisted at the end. I looked off at the horizon, in memoriam to my lost crew. "Rest better, men." The rope squeaked as only good rope can as it tightened with his movements. Out the window I could see dawn was coming up. We had to move. My men were just outside the cabin as I emerged. All four were there, alive.

"Angus?"

"It went well, Cap'n, just as we planned. Not a one woke. Quick and quiet."

"And the words?"

"Some realized. You could see it in their face."

"It's good they should die with the last words they hear is the name of their crime: *Marie Jenny*. Let's go men. The dawn's not far off and we need to be well away from here."

We made short work of getting overboard and swimming to shore. I looked back across the bay. The ship floated in the quiet of the morning, silhouetted on the horizon, the captain hanging suspended from the stern, now quiet and unmoving. I knew when the killing was found out, sailors, being the superstitious lot they are, would never crew her again. The ship would be useless.

We loaded up our packs and started heading west, back to Marquette. The information I had led me there to Peter White.

* * *

Peter White had a quirk. He liked to leave his doors and windows open for the breeze. It was easy for me to slip into his study and wait for him in the dark. It wasn't long and he came through the door, followed by his courier, the agent that executed Mr. White's business. White said a few words and he was gone on another errand.

He walked over to his desk and I revealed myself from the shadows. He gasped and then said, "Talbot?"

"Yes, it's me."

"You look like hell, man."

"That's where I've been and back."

"The ship, the gold?"

"Mr. White, someone knew. We were attacked off of Pictured Rocks and were run onto Big Sable reef."

"The men?"

"Besides me, there are four left. The rest are dead."

"Grand Marais, was that you?"

"News travels fast."

"Faster than a man on foot in the woods."

"We found the wrecker ship that attacked us and killed my men. I also found the name of your traitor."

White's eyes flashed. He reddened in the face from anger. "What do you mean traitor?"

"We were shadowed from the moment we left Marquette. One of the crates was broken into before we loaded it. Though you assured me things were secure on your end, they obviously weren't. The Captain gave up the name before he died. Gold makes men do things they wouldn't usually do."

"Who is it?" He spat.

"He just left here, Comstock, your aide. The captain gave up that he had approached him in one of the waterfront saloons and told him about the gold. The pair struck a deal where the gold would be divided up between the crew and Comstock, of course Comstock getting a larger share than the rest. The captain told me that he never had any intention of giving Comstock anything. Now the gold's at the bottom of Superior deep enough where nobody can reach it, lost."

"Comstock," He bellowed. "I'll fire that son of a whore."

"No, don't. I don't want him suspicious. My men want him."

"I'm sorry how things went, Talbot." He stood up and went to the wall of the study. "I know this won't fix anything, but it's all I can do." He opened a safe that was behind a wood panel and brought out five large bags. They were filled with gold. "Give one of these to each of your men. It will help them start over. After that business in Grand Marais, you can't stay around here. As far as I'm concerned, you and your crew are dead at the bottom of Superior."

"Suits me." I turned to leave. "I can't say it's been nice knowing you."

I slipped into the night and caught up to Angus. "Did you see him leave?"

"Yeah, Peterson and Williams are following him. Dupre is following them in case they get spotted, he can take over and throw off suspicion."

"Let's head for the rendezvous."

Angus and I went to the waterfront and waited near the ore dock. It wasn't long and Dupre showed up. "Have we got him?" I asked.

"Peterson and Williams are watching him in a saloon on the next street. He's putting down the whiskey plenty hard."

"Let's get set," I said.

Dupre led us to the saloon. The back of the building was dark. I told Dupre to go inside and contact Williams and Peterson. I didn't dare, because Comstock would recognize me. I wanted Dupre, Williams and Peterson to follow him out when he was done drinking, and usher him to the back of the building. I knew Dupre would persuade him with a knife blade against his ribs.

It was at least two hours before we heard shuffling feet coming toward the back of the saloon. It was my men and Comstock. Comstock shuffled along in front, pushed and coaxed by Dupre from behind. Williams and Peterson each had a grip on an arm. Angus and I stepped out and Comstock saw my face. In it was his doom.

We pulled him behind the saloon. A cloth was stuffed into his mouth for silence. The next day Comstock was found with most of his bones broken. He had been stabbed twelve times which coincidentally was the number of men from my crew lost in Superior. That wasn't what got people talking. It was the rumor that a name was carved into Comstock's forehead, a woman's name.

White denied knowing anything about it and his reputation held him in good stead. The five of us left Marquette that night. Williams went to work logging near Munising. He had family there. Peterson decided he wanted to go back to Grand Marais to work in the sawmill we'd seen there. Angus and Dupre went to the Soo to look up the old acquaintance MacDonald had told him about. I went to Wisconsin and worked different jobs. Eventually I wandered back to Lake Superior and the Keweenaw, deciding that was where I would stay until I died.

"I've lived my life and death stands near. Now I can die with this tale off from my chest. I've borne my shame and guilt in silence all these years and now, there it is. I thank you, young man." Tears had welled up in his eyes as he shook my hand. He turned and walked out the door. I sat in silence thinking about the tale the old man had told me. The bartender came up and snickered at me. "The old ones they can tell you some stories, can't they?"

Author's Notes – The Wreck of the Marie Jenny

A couple of the characters in this tale are taken from real life. **Angus Macdonald** was an actual trader at Grand Marais. He is often called the first resident, and worked for a merchant in Sault Ste. Marie named **Peter Barbeau**. Macdonald was Barbeau's right hand man and went to establish interests for Barbeau all along the southern shore of Lake Superior. When the pair communicated, they wrote in French the parts they wanted to only be understood by each other. Peter Barbeau (1800 – 1882) went on to be Sault Ste. Marie's first village president.

Peter White is a very common name in the Marquette area and there is good reason for it. Peter White (1830 – 1908) is the father of the region. When he saw a need, he found a way to fill it. He established the first post office and the first bank, and he was a major investor in the first mining concerns of the iron ore discovery. He also served in the Michigan legislature. He was a true community leader in every sense of the word. He also was known for wanting his windows open. He loved the fresh air and felt it kept him healthy. Peter White liked to entertain, and had a special recipe for lemonade that was the talk of Marquette. Near as this author can tell, the large quantities of booze couldn't have hurt its reputation. I've presented it on the following page:

Peter White's Special Lemonade Punch

If made two or three hours before serving, it will improve.

- 3 doz. good Lemons (squeezed)
- 1 Qt. Jamaica Rum
- 1 Qt. Santa Cruz Rum
- 1 Qt. Brandy
- 1 bottle Curacao
- 1 bottle of Chartreuse
- 1 bottle of Maraschino liqueur
- A piece of ice 8 in. square set in middle of punch bowl

One hour before serving the punch, put in

- One quart of strong cold English Breakfast Tea
- Five lbs. white sugar.

One-half hour before serving, put in

- Two bottles of good champagne
- Half dozen Lemons and Half doz. Oranges sliced thinly, Let skin of all lemons go in.

Optional: add two bottles of Apollinaris at the same time the Champagne is put in.

If you do not use it all, skim the lemon peel and bottle it and you can ice and use it another time. It is good to serve at ladies' lunch, if frozen into an ice. It will keep well for months in a cool place if tightly corked.

Poem about *Peter White's Punch* – author unknown

In the queen city of fair Marquette,
On the blue Superior's shore,
Where the wandering stranger is ever met
With a smile and an open door —
Is made a nectar that gods might sip,
Once sipping would call for more.

Oh, wondrous complex is this famous compound,
Which required a full week to complete,
With a dash of this while stirring around
With something to make it sweet,
But it has a queer effect in a cup too much
For the reckless and indiscreet

Thus it did happen to dear Father Marquette, (Statue in Marquette)
He got off his base of stone:
For the night was dark and the night was wet
And he was weary o being alone.
He said, "I will search and try to get some refreshments, if only a
bone."

He walked to a house at the top of the hill —
The gravel his feet did crunch —
In the rear of the house where all was still
Sat a bowl of the coveted lunch.
"Ah! Ha! This will," he cried, "just fill the bill, I've struck the Peter
White punch."

It did fill the bill, and it filled the good priest,
Once tasting he couldn't stop.
"It's a chance of a lifetime to have such a feast,"
And he drank the very last drop,
Nor what happened next did he care in the least,
For the world swung round like a top.

A friend driving by at the end of the night,
Found the very old wight in a very sad plight
And took him back home by the dawn's early light.
He sang his refrain as he climbed to his height.
"I've been (hic) treated wrong and I've been treated right,
But must say that this time you have treated me White."

The Death Trip

We huddled around the woodstove, unable to control our shivering. It seemed it was taking forever to produce any heat to fight off the vicious cold. I looked around at my three companions: Mark, Joe, and Bill, in the semi-circle we had formed around the valiant old heater. We were exhausted, soaked to the skin. We'd distributed the few dry clothes we had left. They hadn't helped much. Already we had nearly died, but the danger was far from over. We were still afraid of falling to the enemy, hypothermia.

Our story had started early that morning. The four of us had come to the Porcupine Mountains Wilderness State Park in Michigan's Upper Peninsula to do some spring fishing and backpacking. Attempting to beat the crowd and the bugs, we scheduled the trip at the park's season opening, the third week in April, also the opening of trout season. Chill filled the air; the temperature was only in the high thirties, but the cloudless bright blue sky promised a good expedition. Snow was evident but only in small, scattered patches. The weatherman had promised "partly cloudy to clear throughout the weekend." We were anxious to get started. The adrenalin flowed. We could hardly contain ourselves. Trout were out there waiting to be caught and we were the right men for the job.

First stop was the ranger's station. From behind the well-worn metal desk, the green-uniformed ranger asked, "Where ya goin' and how long ya gonna stay?" sounding as though he hadn't quite come out of hibernation yet. Mark took out his map and traced our proposed route for him, explaining exactly where we planned to be at the end of each day. The ranger nodded and grunted, then looked up with a smile. "That'll be forty dollars, please." He seemed to enjoy himself at this point. We paid and as we started to leave he called out, "Stop in and let us know when you leave the park."

The ranger's office disappeared behind a cluster of pines as we went into the park. We drove west and south down the boundary road as far as we could in the vehicle to Summit Peak. Our planned route from there ran north to where the Carp River emerges from the west end of Lake-of-the-Clouds and flows into Lake Superior. After hiking to the river, we planned to follow the trail that parallels the river on its journey to Superior. Then we'd continue along the lake shore to the Little Carp River Trail, which leads back to where our vehicle would be waiting. Basically, we intended to make a 21 mile lopsided circle. During our trek we planned to stay for two nights inside park cabins.

After parking the car in the lot, we began pulling equipment out and then strapped on our packs. Mark and I had brought along snow-shoes although it appeared we wouldn't need them. Because we weren't really sure of the depth of snow in the deep woods where the sun's rays were scarce, we decided to bring them along. Mine were small and made of aluminum so they didn't weigh much, but Mark's were wooden Yukon style, weighing at least ten pounds each. Bill and Joe volunteered to trade off with Mark so the load wouldn't be his alone.

Mark and I, experienced packers, managed several trips each year. All of us had spent considerable time in the woods, but Bill and Joe were basically trout fishermen. Camping and hiking with a load wasn't something they did on a regular basis.

Time flew by as we walked along the footpath. We covered several miles and found ourselves skirting around Mirror Lake far ahead of schedule. We guesstimated that we had already covered four miles, but didn't know for sure. Other than the park direction signs that marked trail splits, we had no measurement. When we reached the Carp River, we planned to follow the river bed, because the trail would force us onto the escarpment. Even from our present distance, about a mile and a half, we saw that the escarpment was treacherously icy. The trail we followed had been up and down with patches of snow, making traction difficult. We could only imagine what the escarpment must be like. So far we hadn't had to resort to snowshoes. We were all getting tired, which showed how much winter had contributed to our lack of condition.

Mid-afternoon had us thinking about setting up camp for the night. Our goal was to make the Carp River where it flows out of the Lake-of-the-Clouds. We intended to stick to our plan despite weariness. However, the weather had other ideas.

Robbing us of sunshine, thieving clouds came out of the north. Mark and I looked at each other. We knew what was coming. Bill and Joe weren't far behind us in figuring it out. One of Lake Superior's infamous quick but vicious storms was on the way. This time of year, though, we thought that it would only snow for a short time and then move on.

The leading edge of the cloudbank rolled and churned, boiling and tossing, never holding any shape more than an instant. Then explosive thunder marched over the mountains. The sound slowed only long enough to echo around us. The crashing thunder meant rain, which made me glad that our packs held dry clothing. We were prepared for everything, we thought.

The full fury of the storm was on us with a suddenness that was scary. Torrents assailed us, saturating our clothes with the first wave. Accompanying it was vivid yellow-green lightning that snapped and made the sky appear to have veins and arteries. Much of it stayed above, leaping and streaking from one cloud to the next, while the rest cracked to the ground with a devastating force that could be heard exploding, splintering the great trees that cover almost every acre. Never in my life had I seen such ferocity and sheer force. Then came the hail.

Nickel- and quarter-sized balls of ice pelted us and spurred us on with greater speed. Now we were frantically looking for any kind of natural shelter that we could find, but the deep-wooded forest afforded none. The treetops were high in this area, so at ground level everything was bare. We faced our packs into the now raging wind. This protected us somewhat but we were still beaten up rather thoroughly. We only hoped that it would soon be over. Joe and Bill were looking miserable, but Mark just set his teeth and feet and kept on moving. An accumulation of round pieces of ice under our feet made hiking more like walking on marbles — no fun on the downhill grade. We were coming down the face side of a ridge so we were getting it full into the face. There wasn't anything we could do except keep moving and persevere.

Fighting the noise of the wind, the Carp River made itself audible with its racing, overflowing water. The sound renewed our efforts, though our mood still remained somber. How much longer could the storm last? We were getting bruised from the hail.

We got our wish when we reached the river. The hail stopped, but the snow began: wet, thick, heavy snow. The river banks were covered with previous snow that gracefully transformed into ice that futilely attempted to confine the wildly rushing water of the spring-swollen Carp River. The snow came down hard with a vengeance. In no time, four to five inches were on the ground and it was getting worse. We were all worried. None of us was sure if we were ready for a blizzard that, with every passing moment looked more like it was becoming full scale. Some partly cloudy weather this was. If we could have gotten our hands on the weatherman at that moment, there would have been one less of his kind in the world. At any moment, we still expected blue skies to emerge, sending the storm to other parts of the Upper Peninsula. Our expectations were not fulfilled.

We held a quick council. We were aware of the effects of the lake on weather conditions. It wasn't unusual for freak storms to drop three to four feet of snow in a matter of hours. We prayed that wouldn't happen, but couldn't be sure. We could head back to the car, but it would be hours before we reached it. Possibilities of driving out of this storm were slim. Camping in place was our original choice, but our tents were small nylon pup tents and we were afraid they would collapse under the weight of heavy snow and smother us. That left the one alternative we agreed to follow. At the time it seemed the wisest.

At points around the park are cabins equipped with woodstoves, beds, dishes, usually a handsaw and at least a small supply of dry wood. One is located at the Lake-of-the-Clouds. Its popular location assured us of finding it fairly well equipped. We figured it was one-half to one mile away at the most. There was only one drawback and it was a big one: it was on the other side of the swollen river.

The bridge that crossed the Big Carp River was either washed out or under the wildly swirling waters. The trail simply ended in front of us, disappearing into the muddy overflow with no sign of the bridge anywhere. We would have to find another way.

Searching upriver, we desperately tried to find some passable way to cross. We wound through the trees, wading through the wet snow, crawling over deadfalls. Finally we found a remote possibility. A broad hardwood tree had fallen across the river, creating a natural bridge. It was covered with fresh, wet snow that would pose a real problem, and one point of it was submerged a few inches under the surface for a length of about five feet. Rushing water could easily make us lose our footing. Though treacherous, we decided to try it.

Reaching into Mark's pack, I pulled out a length of parachute line; it's light, thin, and extremely strong. Mark volunteered to cross first, so we tied the line around his waist as a safety precaution. Stepping up on the log, he started across, taking the stance of a tightrope walker. Very carefully he placed each boot, feeling and searching with them, locating places without ice to rest his weight while his arms maintained his balance by stretching outward. The intensity of concentration was reflected in his stiff posture and rigid body.

Breathing was forgotten while he crossed the danger point. Water swirled around his feet about ankle deep, trying to tear him off his unstable position. He inched his way through with the utmost caution while anxiety for the seeming slowness of the operation showed deeply on my companion's faces. Loud sighs came from all of us as Mark's booted feet slipped up the other bank. Joe let out a loud, "Eehah!" and Mark and I exchanged grins and thumbs up from across the river. He found a large yellow birch to tie his end of the rope to. Joe and I tied our side in the same way, pulling it taut. We now had a safety line that ran across the river.

Second to cross was Bill; his tall, slim body ate up the distance quickly. Giving a good demonstration of how to do it easily, he crossed the submerged section with two long strides, getting only one of his feet wet as a result. I followed him, though not as quickly or as confidently. I succeeded without mishap.

Last to cross was Joe. He did well until he came to the danger zone. As he stepped through it, a broken branch came racing down the river, striking his legs solidly and knocking his feet out from under him. He flew into the river, which tried to devour him. Maintaining an iron grip on the line was his salvation. The wildly foaming and churning water flowed around his shoulders and across his pack, creating a drag that was pulling hard, sucking him under. His feet searched but couldn't find the river bottom. His life depended solely on that rope. If he lost it and went in, he could be pulled under the ice flows of the sheet that still covered the Lake-of-the-Clouds. Hand-over-hand he pulled himself through the freezing water. After an agonizing and slow ten minutes emphasized twice by close calls when his hands slipped, Joe came within reach of Mark and me. We pulled him, numb and cold, from the river.

Our first priority now was to get him up and moving as quickly as we could so his circulation wouldn't become impaired, so he could generate body heat. All of us were soaked, but his dowsing had put Joe into a dangerous position. Drastic measures had to be taken, so we decided to abandon two of the packs. I marked their position with my machete by chopping a large X into the tree we laid them near. Mark and I kept our packs plus put on the snowshoes. Bill assisted Joe, who was shivering uncontrollably. Any wasted time was hazardous now. The snow fell even harder while darkness set in, accompanied by a steady drop in temperature.

Blinding snow and cloud cover made the darkness nearly total, so Mark and I took out flashlights. Bill had his hands full with Joe. The depth of snow made us lose the park-designated footpath we'd been following. Fortunately we knew that the cabin was situated directly on the shore of the lake. Mark had stayed there before. So we used the shore as our guide.

We struggled through the deepening snow well into the night. We'd wrapped Joe with one of the sleeping bags, but he wasn't going to last much longer. Almost convinced that we'd passed the cabin, a chance straying of my flashlight revealed it. The discovery was nothing short of luck and we saw it as deliverance. We ran to the door. Mark chopped out the padlock with one of our hatchets while I held a light. Moments later the lock fell away. We pushed the door open and climbed inside. After he helped Joe in, Bill closed the door then latched it shut. All of us were shivering hard, but Joe was complaining about numbness in his arms and legs.

Bill went to work wrapping the limbs, trying to warm them and restore the circulation while Mark and I discarded our packs and snowshoes. Then we searched for dry wood. We found some stacked in a corner already split, but not enough to last more than a couple of hours. One of us would have to go back outside and cut more. After the deluge of rain followed by wet snow, any wood outside needed time to dry out. Leaving Mark to start the woodstove, I took the handsaw, which sat next to the already cut wood. I would have to find enough to get us through until morning at least.

Once again I ventured into the raging wind. I thanked Providence that we were on the sheltered side of the escarpment. Situated on the north side of the lake, the cabin was at least missed by the brunt of the prevailing winds. Those that found their way down were vile. Temperatures had dropped to at least the low twenties. Who knew what the wind chill was? I was cold, colder than I'd ever been, but I knew I was better off than Joe.

Soon, with the aid of my flashlight, I found a tall, standing dead tree. The bark hung in partially attached long strips. It clattered and shivered in the wind. Gusts carried pieces flying through the air. I fell to my knees and started sawing. Dead wood cuts swiftly, which was fortunate. I knew I couldn't stay out in the blizzard much longer. The tree came down with a snap and a whoosh, followed by a loud crash nearly drowned out by the howl of the wind.

Long-enduring shivers shook my body as I stood up to return to the cabin. Blowing snow had obliterated my tracks. Grasping as many pieces as I could manage on one trip, I started back in the direction I thought was right. Between gusts I caught sight of a light. Mark had placed one of the flashlights in a window just in case I had difficulty finding my way back. I dragged pieces indoors until I was certain we were supplied into the next day.

Task completed, I wasted no time in stripping off my wet clothes and replacing them with dry ones. Mark had already changed and distributed dry clothing to Bill and Joe. I finished changing while standing as close to the stove as I could, then joined them in huddling around the old wood-burner. Although dry, we were not warm. The wood ceiling and plank walls bore no insulation. The small stove was hard pressed to warm the cabin. Eventually, it became warmer than freezing, but we still saw our breath in front of us as a reminder of the fate that waited if we let our guard down.

We wrapped Joe, fully clothed, inside a sleeping bag. For four long hours his wracking shivers continued. Finally they subsided. His body temperature started back up. Relieved, we knew we had to stay put and wait out the storm.

The constant snow went on for two days and the wind blew for two more. Our food ran out after the third day, making the return to civilization imperative. Mark and Bill tried to find the abandoned packs, but to no avail. Half our food was stored in them.

On the fifth day I was elected to journey back for help from the rangers. My lightweight snowshoes assured I could travel fastest with the least amount of effort. The day dawned clear and sunny, identical to the one when we started except now the temperature was well below freezing. A crisp, light breeze blew out of the west. Creaking and clacking from frozen branches overhead made the only sound in the woods.

As I came to the Carp River, I met the rangers on cross-country skis coming down off the escarpment. Surprised and elated, I was thankful something was finally going right. They followed me back to the cabin. They'd been looking for us and assumed that we had taken shelter, but wanted to be sure. Our failure to report after four days made them suspicious that we'd run into trouble. The discovery of our parked car confirmed it.

With their aid, we got back to their truck, which took us to our car. They'd plowed it out. We had survived the worst Mother Nature could throw out and, as we left, it was all we could think about. The experience has remained deeply embedded in our memories. Whenever we see one another, we refer to the Death Trip, as we've dubbed it, because that's what it came close to being for all of us.

Wolf Killer

Jacob sat drinking in the warmth of his fire when he felt the eyes. He was good at that, feeling when something was near, watching. His hand clutched his weapon, its silver reflecting moonlight and firelight together in a dancing combination. The creature had been stalking him and he was ready. It would only be a matter of time. The fire blazed bright, the night was heavy and over the great Lake Superior, the full moon hung high.

Suddenly, a flash in the firelight, teeth were all he saw of the beast in the night, a deadly demon, snarling and gnashing. He could smell the fur, the fetid breath. It was the wolf, creature of darkness. He side-stepped its first charge and watched as it slinked around the edges of his camp. Again, it leaped, and this time he caught it around the throat with his left hand. It tore at him, snarling, as he brought his knife into its throat. Blood gushed into his face and a canine scream filled the night. Death was a certainty. Jacob had seen to that.

Then, before him on the ground was an Indian, lifeless and still. A moment before, there had been an animal. "Loup Garou," he spat. But he had known that. This one was his third kill. They were hunting him now, on a trail of revenge and survival: revenge for the slaughter of their brothers, survival because he'd sworn an oath to kill them all.

He'd proven formidable to the creatures. His head had become a prize, one that would elevate a warrior to chieftain. His death had become a matter of pride now, a test of power and strength. They would be coming for him, hard and fast. Half of the second night of the full moon was over and there was only one more night. They had no choice but to kill him now, kill him fast.

* * *

Jacob had first heard about the creatures in Europe. He had been traveling in France when the stories started. Jesuits and trappers who were returning from the New World and New France had talked of them, the Wolf Men. "Loup Garou" the trappers had called them.

Jacob had a reputation as a master wolf hunter. He was called from one town to the next to rid them of a killer wolf. It was a vocation he was proud of, one he excelled at. So well, in fact, that he'd hunted the wolf to scarcity, near extinction. There were no challenges left, no beasts remaining to tax his skill.

It was the Church of France that called upon Jacob. The stories had reached the ears of the Church. Explorers like Radisson and Champlain retold stories of the vile beasts that were neither man nor animal. The reports from the few Jesuit priests who had survived the ordeals of New France related tales as well. Taking this as a confirmation of great evil, the Church was disturbed. Satan was trying to block their path to bringing the word of God to the heathens.

It was purely a business proposition that the Church offered Jacob. As one of Europe's finest wolf hunters, he was employed to exterminate "the abominations of Lucifer." The creatures walked in the guise of the heathen Indian, the godless children of New France. If the beasts of Hell could be defeated, the Indian might have a chance at salvation.

One of the returning Jesuits had sat with Jacob at length and spoken of the tales. "They are from the forests of Lake Superior. There is a tribe of them, not far from the colored rock cliffs of the southern shore. The journey is long and terrible, and evil thrives in those forests. High upon the rocks the Loup Garou can be heard under the light of the moon, howling in the night, followed by the screams of those they slaughter. The victims are found torn to pieces by a savagery that only Satan could conceive."

Jacob had asked the priest, "How do you kill them?"

"Ask the Indian chiefs. They hate the 'Skinwalkers' as they are beasts that pretend to be men. Only they can tell you the ways of killing the creatures. May God have mercy on you." The priest made the sign of the cross over Jacob.

A month later, Jacob departed for the New World. The ship was small and the Atlantic was rough. The trip was less than pleasant. Jacob passed the long horizon-less days contemplating what he would find hiding in the forests of New France. He had heard stories from the gypsies about men that turned into wolves, but in all of his years of killing wolves, no wolf had ever proven to be a man. In the end, he was certain New France would be no different. They'd be renegade animals that had acquired a taste for human flesh. Superstition and old wives' tales filled in the rest.

Land was sighted and they sailed up the vast Riviere de Sainte Marie to Quebec City. From there he would travel to Montreal, the last outpost before the vast wilderness that lay beyond. The thickness of the trees fascinated Jacob. Many sections of Europe and the Steppes region had few trees left. This was something new. The forest had a thick darkness that seemed impenetrable, as if it could swallow a person and no one would ever know. They'd just disappear into the blackness...no trace, no memory of them, simply gone. Jacob became a lover of fire.

The next part of the journey was unlike anything Jacob had experienced before. He was provided passage within a crew of voyageurs. Their immense canoes seated a dozen men and when paddled in a synchronized rhythm, could travel vast distances in a short time. They sang French songs that broke up the routine of the day. Around a nightly campfire they smoked and talked of things and people they'd left behind. The darkness of the wilderness seemed to fade.

Jacob began a gradual understanding of his surroundings. He listened to their stories, studied their habits and learned their woodcraft. Noises in the darkness were identified, his eyesight adjusted so details and movement could be seen. Jacob began to adapt to New France. He worked hard at it. His life depended on it.

The canoe followed a route that went deeper and deeper into the wilds of the New World. Along the way, an occasional stop at the villages of the natives would be a welcome break, a chance to stretch the legs and eat well. The items the voyageurs brought for trade helped inspire the friendly attitudes. The men had chosen a route that avoided territories of the savage tribes. The only ones that crossed those regions were the Jesuits, frequently unsuccessfully.

They paddled hard for a place called Sault de Sainte Marie: the rapids of Saint Mary. There was a large native village there that thrived off the cataracts of the Sainte Marie's River, which blocked all access to the vast and icy Lake Superior beyond. It was along the southern shore of Superior that the Loup Garou were rumored to live.

It had taken them three weeks to cover the distance from Montreal to the village the natives called "Behwating." As they approached, the wild waters of the great rapids could be heard echoing through the dense woods, miles before arriving. The huge canoes landed and natives came out to greet the travelers, hoping for good trades.

A Father Esteban greeted him as he arrived, and led Jacob into the village. "There is an elder here who speaks French and will tell you what you need to know to rid us of these demons."

Jacob nodded and followed the black-robed priest. He stood out in contrast to the people dressed in furs and beaten leather.

The buildings were crude and hand-made, covered with pieces of wood that displayed a shaggy-skinned bark that Jacob had learned was called cedar. Esteban led him toward one. Smoke could be seen rising through the roof as a fire burned inside. Jacob smiled.

The interior was smoky and smelled of earth and hide. Across from the fire sat an elderly Indian. The dim light made the lines on his face seem as deep as canyons. The priest led the way and introduced Jacob to Oshishaway, whose face remained immovable as he motioned for Jacob to sit on the deer skin next to the fire.

Two more natives came out of the dim, smoky rear of the long house and sat next to the fire. The one who sat on the right of Oshishaway was the carrier of the calumet, the ceremonial pipe that produced the smoke that was the blessing of the Great Spirit. As it was passed, each one of them, including Jacob, smoked and smudged, even Father Esteban.

When the ritual was over, Oshishaway began to speak. His French was crude but understandable. "You've come to kill the Loup Garou, the wolf men?"

Jacob nodded.

"They are evil creatures and cannot be killed easily."

"But they can be killed." It wasn't a question. *Everything has a way to die*, thought Jacob.

"Back when our land was young and the Great Spirit first made man and the animals, he made two creatures superior...men and wolves. The Great Spirit loved all of his creations, but none did he prize like wolves and men. He bestowed great gifts on them: intelligence, strength, cunning, and most of all, reason. It was reason that made the wolves nearly equal with man. It was reason that made them realize they were handicapped in their form to develop and live like man. They became angry and jealous and cried to the Great Creator that they should have the form of man as well. They insisted they had been cheated by the Great Spirit.

"The anger of the wolves saddened the Great Spirit who loved them dearly, so he granted them their desire, the form of man. Yet inside, the creatures still lived as animals, as beasts. As a decree, the Great Spirit determined that the wolves, for their arrogance, and as a reminder of the kindness of the Great Spirit, should revert to their true form of wolf at the cycle of the full moon for three nights.

"On these nights they run free in a madness of slaughter and blood. They destroy and devour all they meet. It wasn't always so. For a time, long ago, it is said they lived like the forest wolf, but over time, the mind of the human and wolf became one, the two halves tearing at one another until nothing remained but the madness, the curse of the Great Spirit. During the rest of the month they live as a tribe of people, the gift of the Great Spirit.

"They live alone, these wolf men. None of our people will approach them, none of the clans will trade with them."

"Why haven't you killed them yourselves?" asked Jacob.

"They can't be killed with arrows and spears. It seems the Great Spirit has made them stronger than men. Our warriors haven't been able to defeat them. Many have tried, all have died."

"How do you expect me to kill them, then? I've seen your warriors, they look as strong as any man."

"The Great Spirit came to me in a vision. He told me you would come and I was to give you this." Oshishaway passed something to the native on his right. It moved around the fire until it came to Jacob. It was a metal knife that reflected the colors of the fire. Jacob turned it over in his hand. It was silver.

Oshishaway continued. "It is made of the only thing that can kill them. The Great Spirit knows that the Loup Garou were a mistake. He sends this to you with his blessing. It is made from the metal of the moon and the handle is carved from the leg bone of a wolf. Your French guns are of no use, neither is your long blade, your sword. The Great Spirit goes with you for he no longer loves the Skinwalkers. They are no longer the children he made."

Jacob took hold of the knife's hilt. The weapon had balance and seemed well forged. "It feels like it was made well."

"We've learned some things from our French friends." Oshishaway smiled.

Jacob slid it into his waist sash. "I'll be leaving at sunrise." He stood. He'd need sleep before traveling into the wilderness. Father Esteban stood too.

"I will send two men to guide you into the territory of the Loup Garou," said Oshishaway.

Jacob began to walk out of the long house, then turned and smiled at the old native. "I will show you how to kill them." He turned and walked out into the night, the sound of the Sainte Marie's rapids droning in the distance.

* * *

Light was just gathering on the horizon when Jacob began preparations for his journey into the dark forest. Father Esteban stood next to him as he gathered his supplies. "Take great care, Jacob. God will walk with you."

Jacob smiled at the priest. "Well, it seems I have God and the Great Spirit coming along. I hope they're good at gathering wood for a fire. Listen Father, Oshishaway told quite a story in there. I don't know how much I believe it, but I do know he does. There's something out there, until I see it I won't know what it is for sure." He patted the two pistols in his belt for emphasis. "I take no chances." Jacob then patted the hilt of the knife the old Indian had given him.

Esteban looked at him. "The stories are true. Occasionally, the creatures stray away from their territory. I've heard them. They howl and scream in the night. I've heard the ones they've killed crying out in the darkness as they were dismembered." He had gone visibly pale.

"Whether they are men or wolves or something else, they are evil and must be stopped. I wish you success, my son. I will pray for you."

The two natives whom Oshishaway had promised walked up and led Jacob away from the priest, who watched, hoping this wouldn't be the last time he saw Jacob.

A canoe waited for them along the bank of the great river. They paddled into the cold, icy water of Lac Superior. Jacob noticed how the water seemed to radiate cold. It was a different cold than any of the water he'd traveled through before. It was a deathly cold, a supernatural cold.

They kept paddling and paddling past great dark forests and long sand beaches. They paddled the entire day until they reached a stretch of great sand dunes that stood hundreds of feet high and made camp for the night.

It was a quiet night, one that would be the last for some time to come. Jacob could feel it. The natives were restless and uneasy. The clues told him they weren't far from the territory of the Loup Garou. Neither of his guides spoke French, so it had been a quiet day. Tomorrow would be different.

* * *

Old Greyeye looked up suddenly. Members of his tribe surrounded him and the fire. "The avenger comes. They fear us because we are different. The cycle begins. It is how it should be. We must meet him with skill and cunning. He comes to kill us."

"I am old and have lived long, yet I hope to live longer. The Great Spirit granted us this place and now others want it. It is our home, our place of creation. Tomorrow, when the cycle is upon us, we must hunt the avenger. We must protect our home. We must show him his entrails as he dies."

* * *

Again, they started early, but the guides were more tentative about their paddling. The strokes weren't as rapid. More care was taken with the silence of the paddle dipping. They were getting closer with each stroke.

The natives watched the shore intently. Their eyes were trained to spot movement, any movement. They feared what was ahead. The first night of the full moon was coming that evening and men would become beasts. The wolf men would roam, hunting, devouring.

Ahead, Jacob could see the great colored cliffs. They stood hundreds of feet high, striped with reds, browns, tans and beiges, highlighted with small hints of green and yellow. They were breathtaking. They were forbidding. They were the home of the Loup Garou.

The guides turned the canoe for the shore. The one in front gestured towards a clearing with a pocket of sand for beach. They quickly approached it. The clearing was surrounded by tall pines that disappeared into the darkness of the woods, a darkness that reigned even during the day. Large boulders of sandstone mixed with the trees. There was no wind, no sound of wildlife. Even the sound of the great Lake Superior was muffled to a whisper, creating an eerie silence enshrouding them. The icy fingers of the lake's chill played on their skins as the air moved around them, softly, slowly, caressing them like the fingers of death.

Jacob knew the guides had hoped they had come to this place in secrecy, but he could see they were unsure. Their eyes never left their vigilance on the forest. They gathered wood for a fire but watched for something lurking.

Jacob too was on his guard. If these men were afraid, then there was something to be afraid of. He continued to gather wood alongside them. Whatever these creatures were, if they were related to wolves, they would not like the fire. He was determined to keep it burning large, so that if he kept his back to it, the beasts would have to attack him from the front. It was his strategy from countless wolf encounters, tried and proven deadly to the hundreds, maybe thousands, of wolves he'd killed.

He had it planned. First he'd use the pistols, then the sword and as a last resort, Oshishaway's gift. He'd meet them as he'd always met these creatures, big or small, with wariness and respect, but always ready to spring, always ready to kill.

The night was approaching. The fire was springing to life, and deep in the woods came the crack of a branch. Jacob looked up and realized the guides were gone. Just as well, he thought. They would have been in the way.

They had been frightened from the start and Jacob didn't believe that they were cowards. Standing there, facing something unknown was looking like he wasn't making the smartest choice.

As the moon rose, a long howl began in the distance. Far into the blackness of the woods something answered it. Jacob looked around, watching, searching for movement. He threw more wood on the fire, hoping to build more protection. From the woods he heard a squealing, and recognized it as the death scream of a deer. There was a snarl off to his right. Jacob watched, his eyes trapped between twilight and night vision, details being indistinct, misleading. Off to his left, movement. He turned, a branch cracked. Then he heard it, the familiar low growl...a wolf.

He almost smiled. He pulled both pistols. Let them come! Wolves! More sounds. Snap, growl. Jacob could sense where it was moving now. He couldn't quite see it, but he knew it was pacing, waiting for an opening, waiting for Jacob to drop his guard. Then he could see it. It stood just inside the trees.

As he watched, the creature stood on its back legs, stretched its forelegs to the sky as if reaching towards the moon and then, from deep within it came a long howl that seemed to be endless in its duration. The echo of it bounced around the cliffs repeating itself over and on into the night and the distance. And then...it was answered.

The creature turned and stared at Jacob, still standing on its hind paws, a terrifying visage of a wolf man. It then dropped on all four legs and charged at Jacob, its jaws gnashing with a viciousness he'd never seen, as if it were diseased or insane. He'd seen the madness on canines before, but none with such enthusiasm.

He shot with one of his pistols. The bullet struck the beast in the chest. The effect was as Oshishaway had predicted, the beast was unhampered. He threw the spent pistol to the ground and pulled his sword with the creature almost upon him. He slashed it across the face and side-stepped the charge. The momentum carried the Loup Garou through the fire onto the far side. It rolled and then began to once again stalk Jacob. There was no mark where the sword had cut, yet there was blood on the blade.

Maybe it was a trick of the light, but Jacob's cut had been true. There wasn't any blood dripping from the beast to the ground. Again, Oshishaway had been correct. It sent an ice chill through his bones. The wolf moved around the fire toward him. He grasped the silver knife. As it stalked, the creature watched him, studied him. There was an intelligence behind the eyes, not simply rage unleashed. It was calculated and channeled.

Suddenly it leaped. Again Jacob instinctively moved to the side, to lessen the impact. The silver knife in his hand pierced the flesh. The wolf fell to the ground and rolled away from Jacob. The wound hadn't been mortal, but it was a wound. The knife had worked!

Jacob watched as the great creature once again reared on its hind legs, raised its head to the sky and let out a soul-wrenching scream. It too echoed off the rocks, the sound surrounding Jacob from different directions. Then, the beast reached out its legs like arms and leaped toward Jacob's throat.

This time he took the impact full. It bore him to the ground, snarling and slashing, then twitched and rolled off from Jacob...dead. The wolf-bone hilt of the blade protruded from the chest of the creature.

Jacob rolled away and stood. He reached down to pull out the blade when the change came. Horror and disgust overcame him as the shape of a wolf slowly formed into that of a man. It was an Indian.

Without hesitation he reached down and, with the knife of Oshishaway, cut through the neck and removed the head. Blood coated his hands as he held the head up to the surrounding forest. One hand held the head by the hair and the other gripped the knife, shining blood and silver in the moonlight. Jacob stood, surrounded by firelight, Jacob the Wolf Killer, triumphant once again.

The two native guides had secreted themselves into the woods. They'd watched Jacob's struggle with the wolf man. They thought that Jacob wouldn't defeat the Skinwalker for a time. If that would have happened then the trip would have been in vain, the plan a failure.

But in due course Jacob had won, had shown them what they needed to know. Now it was time to return, to tell the tale, bring the news, the vision had been correct. The rabbit to whom they'd given fangs had killed the wolf.

* * *

Old Greyeye stood on a rock cliff overlooking where Jacob had killed Oneear. He shook with anger and then something distracted him, something on the wind, a scent. It was human. It came from the other side of the clearing Jacob was in. Greyeye motioned for two of his wolf-men warriors to follow the scent, track it and kill those it came from. Next to him stood one of his finest wolf-warriors, Longclaw.

"Kill him," said Greyeye.

Longclaw turned his head to the sky and rent the night with a howl that silenced even the insects. He then disappeared into the darkness. Greyeye looked toward the horizon. It wouldn't be long until morning. Most of his warriors would rest from the cycle until the next night.

* * *

Jacob had picked up his sword and was sharpening the end of a pole with long, stroking hacks; it didn't take long. He stuck it upright deep in the wet sand, then took the head of the Loup Garou and ran the point through it. He walked back to the fire and began to rebuild it. He brought the blaze up again to the size of a full grown man. Once again the fire was at his back.

He knew the night wasn't over. There would be more of them to come soon, of that he was sure. He looked at his blood-caked hands and smiled. He would leave them that way. Washing them would require him to leave the safety of the fire. He smiled again. It was good, let them smell it, let them smell the blood of their own.

Jacob hunched down. There was an extra chill in the air, even as close to the fire as he was. It must be nearing dawn, the predawn chill. He was grateful for it. It kept him alert. Movement in the trees signaled the end of his vigil.

Once again he stood, his stance wide, ready to spring. Another of the beasts wanted to meet death at his hands and he was more than happy to grant that wish.

Longclaw strode out of the woods upright. He was a foot taller than Jacob, and broader at the shoulders. The long arms stretched out in claws that were a mockery of a human's, yet they were much deadlier. Longclaw snarled at him, saliva dripping to the ground as the lips pulled back from the gnashing teeth.

Jacob moved the long-bladed knife back and forth from one hand to the other, his tense nervousness betraying him. As he watched, he knew this beast was different from the first. It moved with greater care. There seemed to be a deeper intelligence behind the eyes. It had the air of experience. It was then that Jacob knew he faced one of their best, one of their eldest.

Jacob watched Longclaw as he moved looking for an opening, a weakness in Jacob's defense. He'd seen what the weapon had done to his brother wolf. Longclaw was wary. He wanted no part of the death it brought.

Longclaw leaped. Jacob was ready. He ducked the outstretched arms, but felt claws rake across his back. He slashed upward, and felt the blade glance off from bone and meat as he missed stabbing inside the rib cage. The flight of Longclaw carried Jacob backward into the fire. He rolled through to the other side, escaping ignition. The wolf-man too had gone through and now stood with a long, bloody gash along its ribs.

A burning branch lay next to Jacob. He grabbed it with his free hand, the silver blade clutched in the other. Behind Longclaw, Jacob could see light on the horizon. Morning was coming. He only hoped it would see him alive.

Jacob brandished the blazing branch between himself and Longclaw, the two moving in a slow dance that was intended to cause the other to make an opening that could be taken advantage of. Longclaw hated the flame and was anxious to make the kill. The wolf side of him asserted itself as he again snarled and growled, then again, he leaped toward Jacob. Jacob defended with the flame. Longclaw was certain Old Greyeye watched, was depending on him to save their people, their homeland.

Longclaw reached out toward Jacob, only to be met with the flame. He swiped at it angrily, sending sparks into the air. Jacob nearly lost his hold, but regained his grip. Perhaps he was only postponing the inevitable. Longclaw could smell the blood of his slain brother and it was driving him to a frenzy. Chaos ruled his mind, his actions. Again he leaped at Jacob.

Sidestepping to the right, Jacob jabbed the burning branch into the wolf's ribs. As he moved, pain shot up his back from his wounds.

Snarling and biting, Longclaw again turned toward Jacob. Longclaw's leg muscles tensed for the spring. Jacob stood square in front of him. It was what Longclaw wanted. He hated the fire but knew it wouldn't kill him. It was time to end this.

Behind Longclaw, Jacob saw the sun break the horizon as the wolf-man leaped for Jacob's throat. He saw the change as the body hurtled towards him, no longer a wolf. The long-fingered Indian collapsed as Jacob buried the silver blade into his ribs. It was his second kill, but this time he'd had an ally...morning. Maybe God and the Great Spirit were watching over him after all.

It was over for the night. He could feel it. He would need it. Food and rest would be his first priorities, in that order. The day would be a welcome respite, for surely the night would bring more attacks. He'd been lucky, they'd only come at him one at a time. If they came at him in force, Jacob was sure there'd be little he could do. He had to admit, he was out of his element. He'd never faced anything like this back in Europe. Wolves there had the intellect of animals, not man. These creatures were something else He believed Father Esteban now, that these were the creations of Hell.

* * *

Greyeye watched as Longclaw died. It shook him to the core. That was two. They were creatures that could not die... and yet they had. Death had always been the companion of the interlopers, the trespassers. Death had always been a sport to them and never a result.

He turned away from the cliff. The Avenger had proved a great warrior, but Greyeye knew time was growing short. Their world was changing, others wanted what they had. His tribe was in the way. The Frenchmen had brought many things to the natives around Gitchee Gumee. They had even brought them a god to replace the Great Spirit. Greyeye shook his head. Someday they would regret it. At least his people would never abandon the Great Spirit.

When night fell, he would end it with the avenger. There would be no more failures. There would be no more deaths among his people.

* * *

The two natives that had been Jacob's guides to the territory of the wolf men ran through the woods with speed that no trapper could ever hope to match. Making no more sound than a deer, they ran toward their village. Behind them they had heard sounds. They were being pursued.

The message they carried was too important. They had to make it back. They had to tell what they knew. If they didn't, everything will have been a waste. Finding another that would walk into the wolf's den, set the plan in motion, to test the truth of the vision and succeed, would be impossible.

One of them was starting to falter, misstep. He looked at his companion. "Run, it is up to you. They will be men now. I will stop them or slow them," he said, grinning, knowing well he had no means of killing them. His companion smiled and handed him something. It was a silver-bladed knife! The companion then continued alone, disappearing into the forest.

* * *

The day had come and gone and now Jacob stood over his third kill. They would be coming now, hard and fast. Half of the second night of the full moon was over and there was only one more night. They had no choice but to kill him now, kill him fast.

Deep in the woods Jacob could see movement, lots of movement. As before, he stood, poised for any attack. Oshishaway's knife was now an extension of Jacob's hand. He had held it for so long and so tight it had become a part of him. A tall sandstone rock stood protruding from the sand beach close to the cliff. A grey-haired old Indian stood atop it.

Several of the wolf men moved below him from the surrounding rock. The old man seemed to be directing the creatures. His arms moved and he spoke the language of Oshishaway, which Jacob didn't understand.

Greyeye stood on the sandstone rock across from the avenger. His tribe waited below him for his orders. He spoke, "Take him. Do not kill him. He is a great warrior, but he has killed our brothers. Tomorrow is the end of cycle. Save him for the pole and the end of cycle celebration. We will dance, we will sing and we will throw pieces of him into the fire as an offering to the Great Spirit. His death shall be slow and painful. He shall pay for killing the brethren of the moon."

The pack fanned out and surrounded Jacob.

* * *

Jacob saw them coming. He was sure they'd kill him now. There was going to be no more of the one-on-one. Jacob had proved too strong. The old leader had lost his patience and was now putting an end to it. It was time to die.

He determined he'd take as many of the beasts with him as he could. He watched as they moved into positions surrounding him. He clutched Oshishaway's knife. Then they were on him.

Jacob slashed and cut, but they overwhelmed him all at once. He was pushed to the ground by the sheer weight of them and pinned. The faces of the wolf demons were over him, hatred and rage in their eyes, yet they made no move to end it. Then he saw the old man standing over him. He said something...and then everything went black.

When Jacob woke, he found himself strapped to a pole. His arms were pulled straight up into the air above his head, tied tightly to the tree. Leather pulled tight when it was wet, now drying in the sun of the day, was causing some discomfort. Around him life in the village went on its way. Off to his right he saw the old man, the one that had led the pack.

He was speaking to three of his warriors, but Jacob couldn't understand the words. His head was ringing from what could only have been a substantial blow to it. They had kept him alive, but for what? This would be the third night of the full moon, the last in the cycle. He pulled on his bonds, testing for weaknesses. There were none.

The old man saw that he'd regained his senses. After parting words to the warriors, he walked over to Jacob. He stood eying him for a moment, and then the old man spoke. It was in poor French, but it was understandable. "The man called Radi-son taught me. You see, we don't kill everyone that comes here," he said anticipating Jacob's curiosity.

Jacob replied, "More of my people will come."

"And more will die and maybe even some of us will die. We are in the way. Your people want to trade with the tribe of Oshishaway. Oshishaway knows our land is rich in the things the French man wants. The men of the new god help him. They send you."

Greyeye continued. "We have lived here since the Great Spirit created man and wolf. We will not give up our home easily."

"These people, your people, are creatures that were not meant to be. You kill and prey on others."

"If we were not meant to be, then why are we here? Like all things, the Great Spirit created us. We do not prey on others, we protect our home. We only kill those that invade our territory. We protect our tribe and our children. Are we really so different?"

"You are killers that thrive on slaughter."

"And you are not? You brought with you something we've never known, death. You've shown us that we can be killed and you've shown those of Oshishaway's tribe. They will be coming now. They know the secret the Great Spirit had kept from them."

"Oshishaway says the Great Spirit told him."

Greyeye hissed and spat. "A great spirit named Esteban! It is he who shows the way of our death. It is he that gave Oshishaway your blade." He held out his hand. It gripped the wolf-bone handle. "No Anishinaabe made this!"

"Esteban pollutes us with his god. Oshishaway desires our beaver and fox. The Great Spirit cries out in pain. Maybe our time is over here, but, if our time is over, then our passing shall be bathed in blood."

Jacob dared a question. "Why don't you change with the cycle? When I saw you, you were in the form of a man."

Greyeye looked around. "These are my children. I was there when the Great Spirit gave us our wish. I was among them that asked for the change." He moved close to Jacob and looked deep into Jacob's eyes. "I am old, and can control the change." He backed away and suddenly Greyeye's arm changed, shifting into that of a wolf's with long, slender claws. "You see, I am wolf!" He ran one of the claws down Jacob's bare chest, leaving a stream of blood as it trailed to his belly. "I need no moon, I need no cycle. I am always wolf, as I am always man." He turned to walk away from Jacob, but turned and spoke once more. "I never knew if I could die before. I thought maybe I would simply fade away. Now I know I will die like other men. For that I am grateful." He walked away then, leaving Jacob to hang and bleed in the sun.

"Where are the rest of you, the old ones?" Jacob shouted after him.

Greyeye did not answer. He smiled as he walked away.

* * *

The day went by agonizingly slowly for Jacob. Flies fed on the blood of the wound Greyeye had inflicted. He was helpless to do anything but endure their constant feeding.

As he hung there, he watched the native village go about its habits and routines. Women scraped hides for tanning while men brought in game and fish for food. The children ran, playing games with sticks, and laughing. Mothers chastised them when they got too carried away or interfered with the hard work of the day. It was like every native village he'd seen since leaving France and beginning his long journey into the depths of the wilderness of the "New World."

France, what he would give to be back there? He had been the master of his domain, the great "Wolf Killer." Why had he given it up? He knew his answer. He'd been arrogant, over-confident in his stature. He was a stranger here, ignorant of what had lain before him, ignorant of what he had faced and ignorant of why. Now he was strung up like a hog for slaughter and he was sure that was how the night would end. Greyeye was saving something for him and he knew it was going to be slow, painful and fatal.

Once again Greyeye walked across the village and spoke to one of his warriors. The native left quickly, and Greyeye returned to his longhouse. It wasn't long before he saw that same warrior with a woman and two children leave the village and disappear into the depths of the forest. They traveled west, away from Oshishaway's village.

Soon twilight approached, and the mood changed within the village. The natives became agitated and restless. Some began pacing while others stood tall and straight, watching the changes in the evening sky. There was a scent Jacob began to smell that overpowered the surrounding pines.

The people of Greyeye's village surrounded the fire that now raged higher and higher as darkness closed, the cool of the Lake Superior night driven away by the flames. They paced around it. As they moved, Jacob could see the fingers growing longer, claws sprouting. Hips shifted into haunches and the hair of the canine filled in, enshrouding the bodies in fur. The air filled with the sounds of bones cracking as they snapped and shifted into the visage of wolf.

They were men, women and children, all changing at once. Greyeye stood next to Jacob, watching his people become their true shape. "We were foolish then," he said to Jacob. "We envied men. Now I just pity them. The simplicity of the life of the wolf, they will always be hunted, you know, by men like you. We cannot live together, even when we are one and the same, we battle within ourselves for dominion. See how the form struggles against itself?"

Jacob remained quiet, watching the spectacle of transformation. Faces shifted and lengthened into the muzzles of the canine. Growls and snarls rose from the throng, claws slashed the air, and then stretched to the sky as they stood and straightened into their final forms. Great chests inhaled deeply and bayed into the night, cries and howls of release, a song of exaltation to their Great Spirit, a fitting tribute from his children. Before Jacob stood the tribe of wolf men, huge and overpowering, yet wonderful in their glory, savagery and grace combined, rare yet vicious beings.

Soon Greyeye would tire of him. His life would end any time. "Cut me down. Give me a fighting chance." Jacob wanted to die on his feet, not strung up for slaughter.

"It is the end of the cycle. We have lost warriors to death and to you. The village will take pieces of you and commend them to the flames. It will be long and slow. It is our way."

Jacob watched two of the children in the light of the fire watching their parents, imitating their motions and cries. It was in this moment that it all began. An arrow appeared in the back of one of the children. It cried and squealed in agony, leaping into the air and then fell to the ground, writhing.

Another, an adult this time, was struck square in the chest and fell to the ground quivering, shaking and then dying. Greyeye shouted to his people and they spread apart from each other watching the darkness, looking to find their assailants.

More arrows, and then the forest seemed to come to life. The tribe of Oshishaway charged at the wolf men of Greyeye. In the firelight and now shining moon, the silver of knives and arrowheads reflected back to Jacob. Leading the warriors of Oshishaway was Father Esteban!

"God is with you," he yelled. He marched forward, with the warriors slashing the throats of those that were wounded and dying with a knife of silver.

Greyeye saw him in the same moment. The priest held a wolf-child by the hair, opening its throat. He screamed at Esteban, "I should never have let you go."

Father Esteban looked across the village and saw Greyeye as he changed. For the first time Jacob saw Greyeye as a wolf. He towered over the rest. The fur shone silver in the night under the glare of the moon. His legs and arms were long and thickly muscled, rippling as he ran at Esteban.

Esteban smiled as he pulled a pistol out of his long black robe. He screamed, "For the grace of God, back to Hell, Demon!" He pulled the trigger.

The bullet struck Greyeye in the chest. He staggered, but kept his feet and momentum. Arms outstretched, claws extended, he leaped.

Father Esteban tried to dodge but stumbled over the body of the now human-appearing child he'd killed. As he fell, he grasped the bloody knife.

Greyeye landed on top of Esteban and attacked him with a vengeance. His hands were a blur as he clawed pieces out of the screaming priest, whose voice finally died in a gurgle as his neck was torn apart and Greyeye pulled the head loose. He stood up, one hand still grasping Esteban's head by the hair, a knife handle protruding from his chest.

He strode into the firelight and walked over to Jacob. Greyeye stiffened as an arrow planted itself in his back. He straightened against the pain and stared at Jacob. He reached with his claws and slashed the leather thongs that held Jacob. Jacob's arms dropped, but were numb and lifeless. He'd not be able to defend himself even against a dying Greyeye.

With a long howl he jumped at Jacob. Teeth tore into his shoulder and then Greyeye died. Unlike the rest of his tribe, Greyeye remained a wolf in death.

One of the warriors of Oshishaway found Jacob next to the body of Greyeye. A great funeral pyre was built and all the bodies were burned, even that of father Esteban.

Jacob was carried back to the village at Sainte Marie's River. His wounds healed quickly and he was anxious to return to Europe. He'd seen enough of the New World.

Oshishaway went to him, smiling and grateful. "We thank you for your bravery and courage. Your god and the Great Spirit truly blessed you."

"Did they?" asked Jacob.

"They are dead. The scourge of our people has been wiped from the great rock cliffs. The Great Spirit smiles and is happy with us."

Jacob quietly spoke. "Is he?"

Oshishaway leaned towards Jacob. He said, "The Great Spirit is old, a new god comes."

"But Father Esteban is dead."

"It is of no matter. Another will take his place. It will be many moons, but one will come. They always do. Since the first one came, they have come. If we listen to their words of god, they are happy and bring us things we want, blankets, knives, pistols and wine, all for a few furs. It is good and the Wolf Men no longer stand in our way."

Jacob turned and left. He would go downriver with the next canoe that would be filled with furs. He didn't tell Oshishaway about the question Greyeye hadn't answered: "Where are the rest of you, the old ones?" Nor did he tell him of the warrior, woman, and children that left the village before the slaughter began. It would be his secret.

Sherman Yetty

Currently I'm working in an all night coffee shop / lunch-counter / gift shop in Grand Marais. Yea, you heard me right, Grand Marais, Michigan; so there's no confusion. I'm the lucky one that got the betwixt and between shift, from dusk till dawn.

I'm the guy that's wandering around the store at 3 AM with toothpicks propping up his eyelids. Looks a little weird, but it works. I was sitting in the front window thinking and watching the world go by. At 3 AM in Grand Marais, there's a lot more thinking than world going by.

I spotted someone walking around the front of the Dunes Saloon and heading toward the shop. Under the street lamp I could see he carried snowshoes and had a backpack, though it looked like one of the old heavy canvas rucksacks.

He came in and sat down at the counter. I offered him some coffee, which he gratefully accepted and cradled in his hands. I offered him some food, but he declined, saying, "I'm not hungry."

He said his name was Sherman Yetty and he'd been on the trail for what he thought was a week. "You lose track of time out there," he mumbled.

I thought, *That's really nuts*, but didn't say it.

It was January along Lake Superior. This didn't sound well thought out to me. He said that everything felt dead out there, the wind, the cold, the ravens. "I feel pulled to be there, like it's something I have to do." He sounded distant as he said it.

I wondered if maybe a bit of hypothermia might be setting in. He sipped at his coffee and I asked, "How long are you going to be hiking? Or is your trip over now?"

"No, it's not over. I'll be out there until I'm done." His eyes looked haunted, little black holes. The pupils were so wide there was no discernible color. "I just came to get inside for a moment," he continued. His hands constantly caressed the cup of coffee.

"What prompted you to do this?" I asked, knowing from his looks that this could be a bit personal.

"Because I have to." Apparently he wasn't going to elaborate.

"Are you following the North Country Trail?"

"No," was all he said. "I have to get back out there. I shouldn't have come in here, but I couldn't resist. The light in the darkness was inviting, a moment of peace."

He stood, and I noticed that he hadn't actually finished his coffee. "Well at least finish your coffee." I hoped to keep him warmed up for a little longer. As he looked at me, a small smile shifted his beard. "I got what I needed from it. How much?"

I didn't want him to leave. Though he didn't say much, I found him interesting and wanted him to linger as he partook of his momentary shelter from the elements. Though I didn't know him, I worried a bit for him. "No charge." At this hour, I made the coffee more for myself anyway.

"Thanks," he called back as he went through the door.

I watched him as he faded into the darkness. I often think of him out there with his snowshoes and his pack. Did he find what he was looking for out there? Did he finish his trip or is he maybe still hiking? Don't know. I've never seen him again. But I know one thing, if Sherman ever does wander by, the light will be on and there will be another cup of coffee for him to caress, another moment of peace.

Close Encounters of the Deer Blind Kind

It had been one of those years, spending endless hours in the hunting blind and not seeing too much. Oh, there had been a few deer that had come in to investigate the bait, but there hadn't been any shots worth taking. I was leaning against the plywood wall of my blind, the side of my face scrunched up against a knot, dozing. I was drifting off with visions in my head of that ultimate buck prancing up to the bait.

Dusk was falling when the blind started shaking uncontrollably. I bolted upright, thinking maybe a bear was attacking, one that had forgotten that it was time to hibernate. But, it wasn't a random, angry shaking and rattling, it was rhythmic.

When I'd blinked the blear from my eyes, I saw the world outside my blind light up as if it were noon. Curiosity and fear that my hastily built blind would collapse caused me to poke my head out of the opening to see what was going on. Above me an intensely bright light shone down, nearly blinding my still sleep-ridden eyes.

'My God,' I thought. 'It's the D.N.R.' But then I remembered that I had my license so I didn't care. The only thing was that there wasn't any noise, no droning engine. It hovered like a helicopter, but it couldn't be.

I had to turn away from the light, it was too intense to look directly into. I heard something crash through the woods. "There goes that buck I've been waiting for all year," I told myself.

I pulled my head back into the still-shaking blind and heard a clinking sound coming from the corner. I looked and saw the shells being ejected from my 30-30 by themselves. It couldn't be the D.N.R., that was certain. Then, as quickly as it had started, everything subsided. The light blinked out.

I looked around. Everything seemed normal again except that the woods were dead silent. My face still felt all scrunched up where I'd been dozing against the blind. I got up. Nothing was going to happen now. There'd be no game for miles. I figured that I'd better replenish my bait pile. It was scattered everywhere.

I bent over and started creating a pile. I found myself molding the bait into a long shape. It got longer and taller. I kept repositioning the apples and creating detail with the grains of the Sweetena. Snapping back, I wondered what possessed me to do this, I'd been lost in it. I'd never spent this much time arranging my bait pile before. It was usually pour and go.

When I got home, dinner was waiting.

"Fell asleep in your blind again, didn't ya?" was the first thing my wife said to me. Nice greeting I thought.

"How'd ya know?"

"Your face is scrunched."

I sat down to one of my favorite meals: pork chops, rutabagas, and pickled beets. I started mashing my "ruties" in prelude to dousing them with butter, but an image started to appear in my mind as I added the butter. It was a vague shadow, but it seemed long and steep. Unconsciously, I started moving my heavily buttered rutabagas around with my fork. I could think of nothing else. Suddenly, I snapped out of it.

I looked up. My wife and daughter stared at me with puzzled expressions. "Not enough sleep in the blind? " my wife asked.

I tried to think of something to say. "Just waiting for the butter to melt dear," I said lamely. I looked down at my plate and the strange mound I had sculpted out of my rutabagas. I just couldn't get that image out of my head. If only I could figure out what it was and why it was there.

I gave up on dinner and went into the family room. The news was on and I stared mindlessly at it. The announcer was jabbering about something on the D.N.R and the Fish and Wildlife Service. But then, there it was. Something in the background clicked. My god, it was a mountain. But which one? What was the story? Where was my remote? I had to turn it up. There it was, shoved down the seat of my La-Z-Boy.

"...From Eagle River north. Everyone has been evacuated. D.N.R. and Fish and Wildlife officers say that the virus is running rampant and could possibly affect the human population seriously. The outbreak occurred in the Brockway Mountain area and could spread to all corners of the Keweenaw. The quarantine is strict with no unauthorized personnel allowed through the blockades."

I had heard enough. I clicked off the remote. I didn't know why, but I knew that the image that was driving me crazy was Brockway Mountain. "Honey, I have to drive to the Keweenaw."

"Why? there's no deer up there. "

"I don't know why. I just have to. It's important."

"You know dear, I'm getting a little fed up with this whole hunting thing with you. The only reason you want to go up there is probably because one of your hunting buddies called and they want you to go out drinking with them."

"No, that's not it. I just have to go and I have to go now."

"What do you mean, now? This is getting stupid. I know what your problem is, You got too much sleep in your blind and now you want to go out and drink."

"No, dear, really." I knew the futility of what I said when I said it, but I had to go and I knew it. Nothing would, or could, stop me. My wife looked at me with THAT look. The one that says 'don't you dare or else.'

"Well, I'm going," I said, looking for the keys to my four-wheel drive pickup.

My wife looked at me dumbfounded, then grabbed our daughter. "I'm going to my mother's and I'm never coming back," she yelled and stormed out of the house.

I thought to myself, "I shoulda had her pack me a lunch before she left." I looked in the refrigerator for something to take along. All that I found was one of my wife's odd-shaped pasties. As I looked at it I realized that it even looked a little like Brockway Mountain. Probably tasted like it too. I left it there and decided to grab something on the way.

It was going on two A.M. when I rolled into Calumet. I drove on, not sure why I was doing this, but knowing that I had to. My thoughts kept returning to and dwelling on that strange happening at the blind. I saw cars passing me, heading in the opposite direction. The evacuation up here shouldn't take too long. I saw flashing lights ahead.

It was a roadblock. There were D.N.R. and Fish and Wildlife trucks parked across the road. Instinctively I knew they wouldn't let me through so I pulled and turned around. I needed a back road or an old logging trail. Finding one didn't take long. I figured that if I made it around the initial blockades I should be alright. Most of their manpower would be concentrated on keeping the curious out.

I bounced down a rutted trail that went in the general direction I needed. I had a compass mounted on the dash of my truck. Bargain bin at the hardware store, ninety-nine cents. The trail twisted through the woods, weaving around, in and out of the rough, rocky terrain. The farther I went, the more determined I was to succeed. Soon I hit a paved road.

A road sign said that I was just outside of Eagle Harbor. I decided to go on to Copper Harbor. There were still a couple of hours until daylight. I didn't want to go on the mountain until daylight. Besides, I had a feeling that I was early. Early for what, was beyond me, but I knew it was too soon.

When I arrived at Copper Harbor, I knew I'd made a mistake. Conservation Officers were everywhere. Every wildlife official in the U.P. was there. What were they doing? Breaking up a poaching ring? Had the R.A.P. line finally paid off? They surrounded me and made me pull over. You'd have thought that I was trying to smuggle all of the venison that existed out of the country. I was angry, but I knew I wasn't supposed to be here. I gave them an earful anyway. That's what hunters do when they see Conservation Officers.

They escorted me into the back of a van. I looked up and saw Brockway Mountain looming overhead. So close. Somehow I knew I had to get up there at all costs. Boy, would my wife be angry!

Inside the van there were others. An old man looked at me strangely. "Fall asleep in your blind?" he asked. "Yer face is scrunched."

I looked at him. "What are you doing here? "

"Don't know. I was just walking in the woods hunting and a light flashed on me. Ever since, I've felt like I had to come here, I just HAD to. All of us here are hunters who had the same experience."

The others nodded. Several were still dressed in blaze orange. "D.N.R.'s gonna ship us back out. There ain't no quarantine. They're hiding something."

"How do you know?"

"Well, when I got here, I was able to look around. There are no dead animal specimens or any kind of portable lab set-ups."

"Well, maybe they had their budgets cut."

"No, I don't think so. What they do have is truckloads of apples and molasses coated corn."

I was incredulous. What was going on here? What are they going to do with that much bait?

I looked out the rear door window. The C.O.s were talking to one of the plain clothes biologists. They were arguing about what to do with us. The biologist was insisting on having us go to the top while the C.O.s wanted everything to be kept official. I had to get away before they tried to ship us out. I heard a loud, "That's final!"

The biologist stomped off, yelling, "But they were invited."

The truck was parked near the woods so that if I could get out, making it to the trees should be easy. Once I was there, they'd never be able to stop me. The inside handle of the truck hadn't been removed so I decided to check it. Unlocked. I guess they figured that we'd just sit here like good little deer hunters. Not me. I was getting out of here, even if it meant getting a padful of tickets written up on me.

I heard the C.O.s getting into the front of the truck. I threw open the doors and bolted. I ran through the underbrush into the woods. The mountain was long and high. I would have to move fast to get to the top.

The picture that had stayed in my mind was so clear that it was like I knew every rock and crack of Brockway. I would have to make my way to the far end of the mountain. There I would find what I was looking for.

It wasn't long before I heard the drone of a plane. It was the D.N.R. looking for me. There were no leaves left on the trees so I would have to stick to the shadows. Those plane spotters can read the numbers off a license tag at a mile and a half. I would have to be good to avoid those guys.

Below me I saw C.O.s searching for my trail. Fortunately, they were used to looking for droppings, not human footprints. They didn't seem to be doing very well.

It was dusk when I reached the top. I had just a little farther to go to get to the observation lot. I knew I would find my answer there. I had a great view of Lake Superior and I could see a storm gathering over the water in the remaining light. The big black clouds rolled and twisted in a circular fashion. Lightning flashed, lighting up the ominous looking mass. "Great," I thought, "a Lake Superior blizzard on the Keweenaw and me exposed 1200 feet in the air."

I ran to where I knew I'd be able to see the observation lot and hid behind a rock. I couldn't believe what I saw. D.N.R. and Fish and Wildlife vehicles everywhere. There were truckloads of bait with immense floodlights shining on them. My God, this didn't make sense. What did they expect to find way up here? The entire section had been repaved so that no ground showed. I wondered if they were expecting helicopters. Maybe they were going to have a giant deer blind flown in to go with all that bait.

I could still see the storm brewing and I hoped that something would happen before it hit. The storm began moving into shore. It picked up speed rapidly. I braced myself for a blast of cold wind, but everything stayed calm and quiet. It was eerie. No wind. No cold, just those churning, flashing clouds. It wasn't long before they were directly overhead. And that's where they stayed. I'd never seen anything like it. Talk about unpredictable U.P. weather!

The flashing lightning grew brighter. The center of the clouds began to part, creating brilliant displays of flashing light and almost creating an urge in me to fill my long johns. The light was unnatural. I decided to move closer to the C.O.s, figuring a fistful of tickets and a van ride out of there might not be such a bad deal after all.

As I came down to the lot, I saw that everyone was looking skyward, watching the eerie cloud phenomenon. A couple of C.O.s carried tranquilizer guns. I stood there, unhidden and unnoticed.

Above us the clouds opened more and something moved in there, something big. As it moved downward, the realization of the truth was hard to absorb. It came closer until it was just above us. It was a spaceship, a U.F.O., whatever you want to call it. A tranquilizer gun slipped from the hand of one of the C.O.s, accidentally lodging a syringe in another C.O. He fell unconscious. Nobody noticed. I didn't care.

The ship kept lowering. It stopped about twenty feet above us. In the bottom of the craft, cracks appeared. The bottom was opening. I was apprehensive, sweating, adrenaline pumping. This was a lot better than hunting. A ramp dropped to the ground in a glare of light.

We waited breathlessly until something moved in the light. Our first look at an alien! It started moving down the ramp toward us. We could see more movement behind. It seemed as if the whole ship was emptying itself of occupants.

The leader moved out of the bright glare. I gasped. Instinctively my trigger finger began to squeeze empty air. The leader was a buck and he was huge. His rack was immense, far beyond anything Boone and Crockett ever dreamed of recording. I never saw anything like it. They don't even tell lies in bars about bucks this big. Now all of the bait in the trucks began to make sense.

The leader reared up, standing on its hind legs. He spoke to us, but he didn't use a voice. The words just came into our minds. "We came to report on the progress of our cousin species. They were planted here millennia ago by our race. We had hoped to colonize this planet and develop it for our kind. We had no idea that another race would plant humans here. You became the dominant species, forcing our cousins to devolve instead of evolve. When we arrived and discovered that instead of ruling this world, they were hunted, mindless, we were distressed and horrified. We decided that our two races should meet so that maybe some of our cousins would be given the chance to advance and grow in the direction they were meant to.

Planted? Cousins? We were planted here, too? The strange twists life takes. Briefly I wondered what it would be like to hunt one of these magnificent beings. It seems a strange thought now. Besides, the license would probably cost a mint. The other alien deer were milling toward the bait trucks.

'Wow! It even works on space deer,' I thought.

One of the biologists moved forward and I followed timidly. This was like stepping into heaven for deer hunters. It was too much to take. The closer I came, the more I felt like I was being drawn in. It was then I knew the purpose of it all, why I was there. They wanted me. They had originally wanted hunters of all kinds to meet with them, but I was the only one that made it. They weren't really interested in the D.N.R. or the Feds. They wanted hunters like me. They had wanted us to go back out into the world to teach other hunters. The D.N.R. realized that if the world knew the truth, they would lose millions in hunting revenues each year. That's why they tried to keep all of us away.

The aliens knew their cousins would be written off as failures. I was their only hope for their truth to get out. But, what the aliens didn't know and had failed to understand was the credibility of hunting stories. Their story, when I told it, would be lost among the volumes of wild hunting tales. Their story, when I told it, would be taken for what it was worth, another shot and a beer.

Cave of Gold

It was a beautiful day to be running traps in the woods. The sun filtered through the trees, creating a scene from heaven. *Heavenly,* I thought, then saw the dead man.

He was propped against a large white pine. The face stared vacantly ahead. I had no idea what to do for the corpse, I'd never come across something like this before. I dropped my pack of furs and approached the body.

Suddenly the head moved and the blue lips let out a gasp. I jumped back, startled. I had really thought he was dead. His eyelids fluttered and he focused his eyes. I kneeled down to see if I could do something for him. I pulled open his jacket and saw where he had been shot several times. His shirt was soaked in his blood.

I opened my canteen and gave him a little water. Hopefully it would ease his discomfort. I didn't understand why he was still alive. It seemed to help a bit and he began to speak. "Beware, they aren't far away."

"Who isn't?" I asked.

"Dan Durbin and his boys. They're after me and I think they got me good."

He reached inside his coat and handed me a folded piece of paper. "Take it. It's what they're looking for."

I took it from him, "What is it? Who are you?"

"Arch, Arch Stanton, A map," he said, "Gold."

It was the thing that had been elusive in Upper Michigan. There was lots of copper, some silver, but gold, that was something that hadn't been given up to the prospectors yet. There were rumors, speculation, and hints about the Marquette area, but here there had been no rumors about the Ontonagon region.

"I found it. It was an old Indian mine. One of Durbin's men got wind of it. Shot me trying to steal my map."

I looked around, Everything seemed quiet. Even the birds. That wasn't a good sign.

"Run, get out of here. If you hurry, they won't know who you are."

"What about you?"

"I'm done for. Just go!"

I shoved the paper into my pocket, grabbed my furs, and struck out across country. I hated to leave him there, but getting into Durbin's business was a dangerous thing. It was well known in Ontonagon county that if you crossed Dan Durbin, you were dead. Dead was not a state I wanted to be in. Behind me I heard a single shot ring out. Arch Stanton was surely dead now.

It also meant they would be turning their attention to me now. There would be at least one professional tracker and all of them would have some skill. This was not a good time to be caught without a gun. I thought about heading for home, but if they were tracking me, the last thing I wanted was for them to find my house and family. No one would be safe.

I had a map to a cave of gold, the stuff that sets men's brains on fire, makes them mad, crazy. I've seen it a lot over my lifetime. Greed, the idea of getting rich without working for it is the dream of most men, and most will do anything for it. Thousands of men had flooded to this place looking for just that, riches. Some had found it in the copper and furs, most had not. I was one who had not. Now I held a map to a fortune.

There was only one thing to do, head for Ontonagon and hope Durbin didn't figure out it was me that cheated him out of his prize. Besides, if this map was real, I would need to come up with a plan, to retrieve it without giving myself away. Gold mining doesn't lend itself to secrecy.

I was on a high ridge overlooking the Ontonagon River. The water churned below as it raced against the jagged rocks at the base of the cliff. The noise was deafening. There was a good view of the country

I'd just crossed. It was early in the year and the leaves were just beginning to bud, leaving the forest floor visible.

I searched hard for signs of pursuers, but I didn't see any. It seemed I'd eluded them. I turned and started back down the ridge. Standing in front of me was a big man. He looked as if civilization hadn't touched him in a long time, if ever. Long, filthy furs covered his body and his hair was matted and had bits of leaves and twigs mixed in.

Having no weapons, I felt at a severe disadvantage. He was twice my size and had the attitude of a bear more than he did of a human. I backed up the ridge as he came towards me.

"Gimme map. I might let you live." He smiled, showing brown and black teeth.

I knew that was a lie. "I thought there'd be more of you."

"Was. Backtracked your trail. Left you to me." He snarled with some spit coming out.

His words stunned me, "backtracked my trail." That would have led them home, to my family!

Horror and anger combined welled up inside of me. I had to find some way to beat this big bastard. I frantically looked around for something I could use. There was nothing and with the cliff behind me, I wasn't going any farther. I let my pack slip from my back.

Durbin's man pulled out a revolver and aimed it at me. It incensed me. "Really?" I shouted. "I'm an unarmed man and you're going to stoop to a gun. What a coward. I'm half your size and you're afraid of me." I laughed at him. In that moment, I went a little mad.

I could see on his face my taunts were hitting him. He growled and spat and threw his gun on the ground. His face was mean as he charged at me. I barely jumped out of the way as his shoulder hit my hip and spun me around. A loose rock lay on the ground and I grabbed it.

He turned as I swung it around and caught him on the side of the head. He then caught me in the ribs with a punch that cracked a couple of ribs. I wouldn't be able to take many of them. I twisted out of his grasp then stumbled, on the edge of the cliff, the Ontonagon River roaring below. I reached out to regain my balance and grasped a part of the fur coat. Feeling my tug, the wild man spun around and a rock shifted under his left foot. Several looks crossed his face in a moment and it all seemed to happen so slowly. His right foot lost its purchase and he was falling backward to the river below. As he was going over I let go of his furs and let everything take its course. His body snapped on the rocks below.

I caught my breath and picked up the gun that Durbin's wild man had tossed on the ground. There were five bullets left in the chamber. One was spent, likely the one used on poor, dead Arch. They would have to do. Any extra cartridges would have gone over the cliff with him. Good riddance I thought. I then began my journey back home. Ontonagon had flown right out of my head. Abigail and Ezra were in trouble.

I was upset with myself. Why hadn't I thought of that? Of course they'd backtrack my trail. I expected they'd keep them alive as bargaining chips for the map. But, once they got what they were looking for, they were all dead. At the moment, I had the advantage, I had the map.

But slowly, a plan was beginning to form in my mind. Like all plans in moments like these, it was a desperate one, but it was a plan. I was going to need some help. Durbin had his men and maybe I could get some of my own.

The way I saw it, Durbin had a disadvantage over me. I grew up here. Durbin and his men had moved in. They did everything with force and violence. I was the son of a French Trapper. My mother was a local native woman. My home is not simply a cabin in the woods.

I went south but with a slight detour to my father's homestead. The news about my wife, his daughter-in-law, Abigail, and his grandson, Ezra, would not sit well.

The years and weather had worn the face into countless lines. Pierre Cadot had been a trapper most of his life, since he was old enough to paddle one of the great voyageur canoes. The market had made him a pauper when it fell apart and now he was poorly attempting to farm what he could. When he heard of the plight of my wife, Abigail, the years fell away from him. Then two had become close and my father was particularly fond of her. "Durbin's boys, huh?

They're a nasty bunch, Sam. People like them shouldn't exist. They're the shit of the earth in the shape of a man."

"Yeah, I'm worried how far they will go."

"Well. Ezra is the one in the most danger, but he's still a bargaining chip. Abbie's merchandise. They'll keep her alive if they can. Chain her up, put her to work. You know how they operate." The seriousness in my father's voice made me worry more.

"Abbie's tough, she can take care of herself. You taught her well." I replied.

Pierre nodded. Years ago, when we got married, I had my father take Abigail under his tutelage and taught her how to shoot. He's a much better shot than I am and trapping demands long days away from home. The Ontonagon is dangerous country and women are prey for men like Durbin.

"I'm headed to the house and finish this." I said and headed back into the woods.

It was at least an hour before I reached the treeline that surrounded my house. It was dusk and I could see kerosene lamplight coming from inside. Everything seemed quiet, so I was sure there was a trap waiting. It was too perfect, with the livestock put away. Silence hung heavy. They were here.

I worked my way toward the house. I could see shadows moving against the curtains. They were waiting for me and I wasn't going to disappoint them. I shouted "Hallo, Abigail, Ezra, I'm home." I stepped out into the yard in front of my house.

The door flew open and one of Durbin's men stood there. "We know you got the map. We got your wife and kid. If you want them to stay alive, give us the map."

Another of Durbin's men came to the door and whispered something to the other and went back inside. Now I knew there were at least two of them, probably three. "What if I don't?"

"We shoot the kid first. We said we'd keep the woman alive, but the woman's ours." He laughed.

I threw out the only card I had. "I want to talk to Durbin myself."

"Why should he bother? All we have to do is shoot you and take the map."

"That'd be true if I had it on me."

This caused some confusion on their part. Obviously Durbin wasn't hiring for brains. This possibility had apparently not occurred to them. "Smilin' Dan Durbin don't talk to nobody. He does the talkin'."

"I want to deal, isn't that better than killing an entire family?" I sounded desperate. I wasn't.

The pair thought about it for a minute, then they shook their heads, "No, we like that. Pays good, sheriff works for us anyways. What's not to like?"

Out of the corner of my eye I saw movement, over near the barn. I kept talking.

"Well, you might get some small satisfaction…"

"No, it's a lot."

"My point is you still won't have the map. With me dead, you'll never find it."

"We'll see," said the first of Durbin's men. He turned and yelled, "Karl, bring the boy out here."

This was the moment of truth. My hand clinched on the revolver I held. This was probably going to get ugly.

There was no answer from Karl. There was no Ezra. The "leader" looked at the man next to him. "Check on Karl, Paddy."

Paddy turned and went inside. A shot rang out. As the "leader" turned to react to the sound of the gunshot, the door flew open and Abigail came through with a revolver in her hand and shot the surprised man in the head. She then shot him twice more as he fell. "Threaten my family will ya, dog shit piece of dirt!"

Pierre poked his head out from around the barn. He had Ezra. Abigail ran over and hugged the dark-haired, blue-eyed son of ours.

"Still don't know why you had to give him that stupid name." mumbled Pierre.

"I like it," Abigail yelled at him.

It had been an ongoing point of contention between the two of them, since Ezra was born. Pierre said, "I went in around the back. I snuck up on the man guarding Abbie and Ezra and strangled him. When I cut her loose she shoved Ezra at me and insisted on the gun.

Never won an argument with her yet, figured it wouldn't start now. You must have waited and shot the other one when he came into the back. "

Abigail nodded and turned her attention toward me. "What the hell horseshit are you dragging us through now? These shitpiles broke into the house ranting about you and some map."

I looked at my father. "You had to teach her to curse, too?"

He grinned, "My wedding gift to you, a woman who can defend herself and curses like a sailor."

"Thanks," I turned to Abigail and told her the day's events leading up to the moment.

"Well, I'm pissed," she responded. "They threatened me, my son, and all over a damn map. I say we go put a boot up Durbin's ass."

"She makes a good point," replied Pierre, "They aren't going to leave us alone until we resolve this."

"That's certain. I'd be willing to bet they sent off a message to Durbin, letting him in on everything, except what we just did here. He probably figured they have it all sewed up. That's our advantage. It'll be awhile before he realizes his men aren't coming back."

My father looked at me hard. "You realize, he'll be coming just over killing his men. He'll see it as personal now. He's gonna throw everything he's got at us."

"And that's substantial," I put in.

"Listen, I don't care how many men this nob has got. If we're not safe until Durbin's gone, then I only see one solution. He's gotta go one way or another. I'm gonna wipe that shit eatin' grin off his face." Abigail looked lovingly at the revolver she was holding, mumbling, "They tied me up, threatened to shoot my son in front of me. I'm not gettin' over that anytime soon." She then turned to Pierre, "Take Ezra to Lily. She can watch him until this is over."

"I hate that name," mumbled Pierre.

Lily was my mother, Ezra's grandmother and Pierre's wife. We were assured she would give up her life before the boy. She knew how to use a gun, too.

Abigail looked at me, "Cave of gold, huh."

"That's what he said. An old Indian dig. It would make sense. I don't know much about it but I do know our local Indians didn't like gold, it was copper they wanted. Easier to work into things. Gold didn't work as well, too soft. They would have abandoned it with the gold still there."

"So you think this could be real?"

"Don't know until we follow the map and look for ourselves. First we have to take care of Durbin."

* * *

Smilin' Dan Durbin was an evil man. He had amassed a fortune through extortion, prostitution, robbery and murder. If you opposed him or spoke out against him, there were always consequences. The sheriff and his deputies worked for him. Whatever he ordered, they covered it up. They were compensated very well for their efforts. And if you developed a streak of conscience, your usefulness was over.

Smilin' Dan got his nickname because he always smiled when he talked, no matter what was coming out of his mouth. The only time he seemed to experience true joy was when he was ordering someone else's demise.

Smilin' Dan also had a quirk, he never left his stockade. He had created a small fort outside of Ontonagon where he ran most of his operations. Gambling, prostitution, all happened behind these walls.

Most of my life, I had steered clear of Durbin and his operations. It just seemed like a bad deal all the way around for me. The life span of one of his employees was very limited. They were well paid, but they were expected to spend it in Dan's brothels and poker games. No, it always seemed like bad deal to me.

The only way we were going to beat Dan would be with some help. I was going to have to have my father, Pierre call in some favors.

For years Durbin's men had been kidnapping local native women and using them as slaves in their brothels. They picked on Indians because if they complained no one would listen to them. Their women were easy pickings for Durbin. This had been going for years and the natives were tired of it. It might not take much of a push to get them to join our cause. Pierre had been good to them through the years and my mother Lily was the previous chief's daughter. We could make it about family, about revenge, about ridding ourselves of an evil forever, we could make it about getting the people that had been taken back. There would be no need of mentioning any...cave of gold.

If Pierre could get the tribe to help, then we might just have a chance. We could drive Durbin and his men out once and for all. The rest would take care of itself. The problem was that Durbin had a very good thing here and he wasn't going to leave voluntarily or quietly. It would have to be over his dead body.

Pierre left to sit and smoke with the tribal elders and convince them of our cause. My plan included an idea I'd read about that was going on down south after the civil war: night riders. Hooded men rode with torches to harass the blacks who were trying to make a life for themselves. My idea was for the Indians to hood and cloak themselves so that in the aftermath, no blame could be placed on them. No one would know who really did it. For all Ontonagon would know, it would be a rival gang that drove them away. With the law in Durbin's pocket, it seemed to me it was time for some drastic measures: native night riders. I liked the sound of that.

Pierre returned with close to fifty natives, many having lost someone to Durbin's men. They were eager for a payback. Many hoped that loved ones might still be alive inside. Tonight would tell the tale. Abigail had reluctantly agreed to stay with Lily and Ezra until the raid was over. If we failed and my father and I went down, they would need each other to carry on.

* * *

Fifty natives dressed in black were mounted outside our house. It was an amazing sight. The plan was that Pierre and I would walk directly to the gate and demand to see Smilin' Dan to bargain for the map. When we were brought inside, that would be the signal for fifty natives to begin setting the stockade on fire. Once the fires were set, the place should erupt in chaos, giving us our opportunity to finish off Dan. It was a good plan, and I thought it had a good chance of working.

Pierre and I approached the gate cautiously. We were both worried we wouldn't get inside alive.

The stockade itself was a vertical log wall that completely surrounded the encampment. The gate was open but there were two wolves staked out, which had chains long enough that they couldn't quite reach someone walking through. They growled and snapped at us as we approached the two guards on the other side. They wore long furs like the wild man that had chased me back at the cliff. This pair was smaller.

"We want to see Dan," I said.

"Dan don't see anybody."

"He'll want to see us. I'm Sam and that's Pierre Cadot. We came to talk about a map."

The two held torches close to our faces, looked at each other and nodded. "There's a lot of people looking for you two."

"So we've heard. Take us to Dan."

"Sure," muttered the man on the right. "Not every day you see men walking into their own funerals."

They led us to a log shack that was Dan's "Office." As we came through the door, I was shaken to the core. Dan sat there with his disgusting grin on a huge wooden chair that looked remarkably like the throne he imagined it to be. Surrounding him was several of his slave prostitutes and one of them was Abigail!

"How the hell?" I thought, but tried not to show it.

Dan sat up as we entered and I tried not to give away my surprise at seeing Abigail. This complicated things. "Gentlemen," Dan said with that smile, "We've been looking for you."

"The rumors are everywhere," said Pierre. "We want to deal."

Dan held up a cup he'd been swilling rye in. Abigail promptly filled it. Throwing back a big swallow, he commented casually, "Why should I deal? You're here." He opened his arms in a flourish as he looked around at his tiny kingdom. There is nothing you can do, nowhere you can go. I will always find you." He leaned forward and coughed a bit.

Outside, the wolves were howling, followed by shouts. "What's going on?" yelled Dan.

I knew the night riders had begun their raid.

One of his men leaned in, "Fires!" he shouted. They're setting fires all around."

Dan rose in a rage and shouted "You two'" pointing his finger at Pierre and me, "You're responsible for this." He then burst into a spasm of coughing that he couldn't stop. A look of realization came over his face. Red foam started to come out of his mouth and Dan was no longer smiling.

Abigail came running over to me. "What did you do?" I asked.

"Poison—arsenic. Bastard! You never know what a mother will do when her child is threatened." She grinned at me. "I really wanted to blow his damn brains out, but then I realized some poor woman would have to clean up the mess so I tried poison. Much cleaner."

We had to get out of there. As I predicted, chaos ensued during the attack and fire. Hooded men and Durbin's men were running in all directions. Men and animals slipped in the mud in an effort to be somewhere else. The fires danced and cast bouncing lights in the chaos. Eventually we worked our way out and away from the burning stockade.

Many were rescued that night. There were only charred remains of the stockade.

* * *

With Durbin dead, it was time to see if the map was real. Pierre and I decided to follow the map ourselves but Abbie wasn't having it. "I risked my life for this map as much as either one of you did. I'm going along."

The map was well detailed, and led us into a region that had been dubbed the "Gogebic Ridge." It was a series of high bluffs that were near the Ontonagon River not far from where Alexander Henry, the explorer, had discovered the Ontonagon copper boulder that the local natives used to worship. To date, it is the largest piece of copper found. This gave me great hope that the map was real. If copper was here, gold could be too, even silver.

Following the big river wasn't easy. We started out paddling a canoe to get as far upriver as we could. It was early in the year and the water was still high, and after portaging a long series of rapids we decided to abandon the canoe. The forest was thick and tall. Great pines rose all around, nestled in the long stretches of rock bluff.

The map led up and over ridges, and the hike was hard and long. Eventually we came to the area where the cave was marked. All three of us were excited when we saw holes in the ground as we approached. Shallow pits were everywhere. The Indians had indeed worked this place hard looking for copper.

The map said that there would be a stream ahead with a cascading waterfall. The cave was supposed to be next to it. This would be it. What it all came down to, the fighting, the death, the fear, a cave of gold waited ahead.

We walked around a large rock outcrop. We could hear the roar of the falls ahead. Abigail looked at me and grinned. "Let's hope it was all worth it, Sam."

"Just getting rid of Durbin made it all worth it," I replied.

Pierre warily walked ahead of us. Something had set him off, and he motioned us back. We walked toward the falls after him. I knew my father and this stance meant there was danger.

"Ugh, what's that smell?" Abigail twisted her face in a repulsive look.

"Bear, dear, that's what one smells like," I answered. There was no mistaking it. It was a black bear and it was beginning to occur to me that the cave of gold might also be a bear den!

If there is a bear, then it would have just come out of hibernation. It would be hungry and groggy. In other words, very unpredictable.

With a large cliff face to our left and a fast flowing stream to our right, we walked toward the falls. I tried to get Abigail to stay behind me, but she wasn't having any of it. She moved ahead right on Pierre's tail. I watched behind, in case the bear wasn't actually in the cave. They tend to come up behind their prey.

Ahead I could see a hole gaping in the cliff face. It wasn't like the ground pits we had seen on the way in. It went straight into the cliff. There had been some major work done on this mine.

My thoughts distracted me. It is surprising how quiet a black bear can be.

He jumped on my back. I had been completely oblivious to his charge until I felt the impact, then the teeth and claws. It was fortunate that I was wearing a rucksack and a thick wool coat that dulled the force of the attack. I rolled with the beast, which seemed to claw and bite with savagery that was nearly impossible to defend against. Just as importantly, the way we were moving together, I was keenly aware of the fact that neither Pierre or Abigail would have a clean shot. I figured I was on my own until I could separate myself from the bear.

His teeth sunk into my sleeve, tearing the shoulder loose from the threads. He continued to claw at my back as we rolled together. Unknown to me at the time, Pierre had picked up a large, thick piece of tree branch and had worked his way over near me.

The bear twisted me so that he was on the top. Suddenly there was a resounding thud as the branch collided with the side of the bear's head. It pulled the bear's attention from me to him. It was then that Abigail unloaded six shots into the beast dropping it right there.

"Sam, are you all right? Scared the shit out of me," she said as she knelt down next to me.

"Scared the shit out of me, too. Nice shooting by the way, you're a treasure." I replied. "I'll be alright as soon as I catch my breath. Nothing broken, some bleeding and soon to be lots of bruising."

I was breathing hard and checked myself for damage from the bear's attack. The thick wool coat had undoubtedly saved my life. I'd gotten scratched on my back and bitten on my arms, but nothing had been damaged permanently.

I turned my attention back to why we were there. The cave was in front of us and we needed to know. *Is the map real? Is there a cave of gold?*

I stood up, knowing I'd be really sore tomorrow, but I put that behind me as we moved forward. We still approached the cave entrance warily. Pierre had some candles in our gear. We struck matches on the rock and got them lit. The cave didn't go in a long way, but it didn't need to. The color of gold glittered everywhere. It ran through quartz on the walls and seemed to well in large pools in the rock.

We marveled in amazement as all three of us realized it was true. The map really had led us to a cave of gold. We took a hammer and chisel that we had brought along in our rucksacks. We would have to take samples back to have them assessed and assayed and file a claim on our find. The three of us danced our own strange erratic jig as we celebrated our newfound fortune.

In Houghton, we searched out a local mining office. Since mining copper had begun in the Keweenaw, the town of Houghton had established itself as the region's experts on everything mining. The place was flush with geologists. They were everywhere and we would be able to file a mining claim here too.

As we entered the office of a local geologist, we pulled out our rock samples and placed them on the counter. Our excitement rose inside as the geologist picked them up and looked them over. He scowled and then said "I'll be right back. I need to run some tests."

We watched as he went through a curtain into a room in the back. Abigail leaned over to me. What's he doing?"

"Probably testing for purity. It'll tell us how rich we are." I was grinning a smile I couldn't wipe off my face.

Pierre was nervously pacing by himself off in a corner.

It wasn't long and the geologist came back out. "I was pretty certain of the results but I wanted to run a couple of tests to be sure."

"Well?" we all three said in unison.

"Hmmm., I got bad news for you. There's gold here, but it's about 85% pyrite."

"What do you mean," I said.

"There's some gold here, flecks of it in the quartz, but most of what you have here is Iron Pyrite, 'Fools Gold.' They are frequently found together. Unfortunately the real gold content here is so small that it would take you a year to mine enough for a good steak dinner."

We looked at each other and Pierre began to laugh. "Well, we're no worse off than we were before, except now, no one has to put up with Smilin' Dan Durbin anymore."

He was gone, the corruption and crime would stop now. At least until the next crook moved in.

Author's Notes – Cave of Gold

The character of Smilin' Dan Durbin is modeled after a real character named **Dan Dunn**. He had a stockade located near Seney, much like the one I describe. He was a local saloon owner who moonlighted in prostitution and extortion on the side. His solution for those that got in his way was murder. In 1891, he was shot dead in a hotel lobby in Trout Lake.

The stockade portrayed in the story was toned down from the reality. There were several of them located around the Upper Peninsula including the Ontonagon region. Chase S. Osborn, former governor of Michigan, writes a graphic description of one of these places that was located in Florence, Wisconsin, and speaks of a crime racket that extended for a couple of hundred miles in every direction. He writes in his book *Iron Hunter* that the crime group in Florence was responsible for Dan Dunn's murder. He also states that women were kidnapped from rural areas like farms in Ohio and Indiana and then brought to the north, locked in these stockades and then "broken." All U.P. frontier women were in danger from these marauders, hence the rough edges on the character of Abigail.

About the Author

Mikel B. Classen has been writing about northern Michigan in newspapers and magazines for over thirty-five years, creating feature articles about the life and culture of Michigan's north country. He's written about Upper Peninsula history, travel, outdoors, the environment and many other subjects. A journalist, historian, photographer and author with a fascination of the world around him, he enjoys researching and writing about lost stories from the past. Currently he is Managing Editor of the *U.P. Reader*.

Classen makes his home in the oldest city in Michigan, historic Sault Ste. Marie. He is also a collector of out-of-print history books, historical photographs and prints of Upper Michigan. At Northern Michigan University, he studied English, history, journalism and photography. He lives with his wife, Mary L. Underwood, and his Labrador retriever, Gidget.

His books include

- *Au Sable Point Lighthouse, Beacon on Lake Superior's Shipwreck Coast* (History Press, 2014)
- *Teddy Roosevelt and the Marquette Libel Trial* (History Press, 2015)
- *Journeys into the Macabre* (NetBound Books)
- *U.P. Reader (Volumes 1-5)* as Editor (Modern History Press)
- *Points North: Discover Hidden Campgrounds, Natural Wonders, and Waterways of the Upper Peninsula* (Winner of the State History Award)

To learn more about Mikel B. Classen and to see more of his work, go to his website at **www.mikelclassen.com**

The U.P. Reader:

Bringing Upper Michigan Literature to the World

Michigan's Upper Peninsula is blessed with a treasure trove of story-tellers, poets, and historians, all seeking to capture a sense of Yooper Life from 'settlers' days to the far-flung future. Now, U.P. Reader offers a rich collection of their voices that embraces the U.P.'s natural beauty and way of life, along with a few surprises.

The annually published volumes take readers on U.P. road and boat trips from the Keweenaw to the Straits of Mackinac. Every page is rich with descriptions of the characters and culture that make the Upper Peninsula worth living in and writing about. U.P. writers span genres from humor to history and from science fiction to poetry. This issue also includes imaginative fiction from the Dandelion Cottage Short Story Award winners, honoring the amazing young writers enrolled in the U.P.'s schools.

Whether you're an ex-pat, a visitor, or a native-born Yooper, you'll love U.P. Reader and want to share it with all your Yooper family and friends.

Available in paperback, hardcover, and eBook editions

To learn more: visit www.UPReader.org

Discover Your U.P. in *Points North* by Mikel Classen

This book has been a labor of love that spans many years. The love is for Michigan's Upper Peninsula (U.P.), its places and people. I've spent many years exploring the wilderness of the U.P., and one thing has become apparent. No matter what part you find yourself in, fascinating sights are around every corner. There are parks, wilderness areas, and museums. There are ghost towns and places named after legends. There are trails to be walked and waterways to be paddled. In the U.P., life is meant to be lived to the fullest.

In this book, I've listed 40 destinations from every corner of the U.P. that have places of interest. Some reflect rich history, while others highlight natural wonders that abound across the peninsula. So many sights exist, in fact, that after a lifetime of exploration, I'm still discovering new and fascinating places that I've never seen or heard of. So, join in the adventures. The Upper Peninsula is an open book--the one that's in your hand.

"Without a doubt, Mikel B. Classen's book, *Points North*, needs to be in every library, gift shop and quality bookstore throughout the country--particularly those located in Michigan's Lower Peninsula. Not only does Classen bring alive the 'Hidden Campgrounds, Natural Wonders and Waterways of the Upper Peninsula' through his polished words, his masterful use of color photography make this book absolutely beautiful. *Points North* will long stand as a tremendous tribute to one of the most remarkable parts of our country."

--Michael Carrier, author Murder on Sugar Island

Learn more at www.PointsNorthBooks.com

CPSIA information can be obtained
at www.ICGtesting.com
Printed in the USA
LVHW080912120621
690072LV00002B/63